DATE DUE

ALSO BY

CARLO LUCARELLI

Carte Blanche
The Damned Season

VIA DELLE OCHE

Carlo Lucarelli

VIA DELLE OCHE

*Translated from the Italian
by Michael Reynolds*

Europa
editions

Europa Editions
116 East 16th Street
New York, N.Y. 10003
www.europaeditions.com
info@europaeditions.com

Copyright © 1996 by Sellerio Editore, Palermo
First Publication 2008 by Europa Editions

Translation by Michael Reynolds
Original Title: *Via delle Oche*
Translation copyright © 2008 by Europa Editions

Library of Congress Cataloging in Publication Data is available
ISBN 978-1-933372-53-2

Lucarelli, Carlo
Via delle Oche

Book design by Emanuele Ragnisco
www.mekkanografici.com

Prepress by Plan.ed – Rome

Printed in the United States of America

CONTENTS

Translator's Note

Dottore: In Italy, the title "dottore" (first appearing on p. 27) is conferred on anyone who has earned a university degree, in any field of study, not just medicine. The position of police commissario requires a university degree, thus, as means of showing respect, "dottore" is often used in place of commissario. Early in the book, Commissario De Luca explains why his case is slightly different.

Decima Mas: An elite corps of the Italian navy active during the fascist period. While officially dismantled in 1943, the name and insignia were utilized by the Italian Social Republic from 1943 until the end of the war, and the corps became an instrument of terror in the hands of Nazi Germany and the fascist Salò Republic.

The *Muti*: A military corps (named after Ettore Muti, secretary general of the Italian Fascist party from 1939 to 1940) responsible for field operations, policing, and investigations in the Italian Social Republic.

Case Chiuse: The practice of prostitution within licensed bordellos was legal in Italy until 1958. The Italian state regulated and policed many aspects of the industry, including: prices; the rating of bordellos (ranging from "luxury" to "common"); where and when such establishments could and could not operate; the mandatory turnover of staff every fifteen days; and the fact that doors and windows facing the street had to remain closed, hence the name by which legalized bordellos were also known, "case chiuse" or "closed houses."

Prefect: Appointed by the Minister of the Interior, the prefect is a representative of the national government in a given territory. All local branches of government agencies, including law enforcement and public safety agencies, are answerable to the prefect.

PREFACE

I ran across a strange character who in a certain sense changed my life.

He was a policeman who had spent forty years in the Italian police, from 1941 to 1981, when he retired. He had started in the fascist political police, the OVRA, a secret organization the meaning of whose very acronym was never known with certainty. As an "ovrino," he told me, his job was to tail, to spy on, and to arrest anti-fascists who were plotting against the regime. Later, still as an ovrino, he was to tail, to spy on, and to arrest those fascists who disagreed with fascism's leader, Benito Mussolini. During the war, his job went back to tailing, spying on, and arresting anti-fascist saboteurs, but toward the end of the war, when part of liberated Italy was under the control of partisan formations fighting alongside the Allies, my strange policeman friend actually became part of the partisan police. As he was good, he told me, he had never done anything particularly brutal and the partisans needed professionals like him to ensure public order and safety. Naturally, his duties included arresting fascists who had stained themselves with criminal acts during the war. Several years later, when, following elections, a regular government was formed in Italy, our policeman became part of the Italian Republic's police; his job, to tail, to spy on, and to arrest some of those partisans who had been his colleagues and who were now considered dangerous subversives.

That encounter, and the studies I was undertaking at that moment, opened my eyes to a period that is fundamental in the history of Italy: strange, complicated and contradictory, as were the final years of the fascist regime in Italy.

Benito Mussolini and the fascists took power in October, 1922. For twenty years, the regime consolidated itself into a ferocious dictatorship that suspended political and civil liberties, dissolved parties and newspapers, persecuted opponents and put practically all of Italy in uniform, like what was happening in the meantime in Hitler's Germany. The outbreak of World War II saw Italy allied with Nazi Germany, but a series of military defeats, the hostility of a people exhausted by the war effort and the landing of the Anglo-American forces in Sicily in 1943 brought about the fall of the fascist regime. Mussolini was arrested and, on September 8, the new government decided to break the alliance with Hitler and carry on the war alongside the Allies.

At this point, Italy splits in two as the German Army occupies that part of the country not yet liberated by the advance of the Anglo-American forces and puts Benito Mussolini in charge of a collaborationist government. This is one of the hardest and most ferocious moments in Italy's history. There is the war stalled on the North Italian front, where there is fierce fighting, for at least a year. There is dread of the *Brigate Nere*, the Black Brigades, and the formations of the new fascist government's political police who, together with the German SS, repress sabotage activities and resistance by partisan formations. There is, above all, enormous moral and political confusion that combines the desperation of those who know they are losing, the opportunism of those ready to change sides, the guilelessness of those who haven't understood anything and even the desire for revenge in those who are about to arrive.

Only a couple of years, until April, 1945, when the war in Italy ends, but two ferocious, bloody, and above all confusing years, as I learned thanks to my studies and the accounts of my policeman friend. In Milan alone, for example, there were at least sixteen different police forces, from the regular police, the "Questura," to the Gestapo, each doing as they pleased and sometimes arresting one another.

But above all, I understood one thing from that encounter. For, after having heard that man recount forty years of his life in the Italian political police, during which with every change of government he found himself having to tail, to spy on, and to arrest those who had previously been his bosses, the question came spontaneously to me: "Excuse me, Maresciallo, but . . . whom do you vote for?" And he, with equal spontaneity, responded: "What does that have to do with it? I'm a police-man." As if to say: I don't take political stands. I do. I am a technician, a professional, not a politician.

At that point, I thought that there are moments in the life of a country in which the technicians and the professionals are also asked to account for their political choices and non-choices. I thought about what my policeman friend would have done if things had gone differently. And to ask oneself "what would have happened if" triggers the idea for a novel.

So I started writing *Carte Blanche.* I invented Commissario De Luca, protagonist of *Carte Blanche, The Damned Season* and *Via delle Oche,* and lost myself in his adventures.

And I never did write my thesis.

Carlo Lucarelli

VIA DELLE OCHE

for Tecla

"The Italian people will soon be asked to choose not so much between
two political groups or two different socio-ideological notions,
but between Russia and the West . . ."
Giornale dell'Emilia [1]

"We want to preserve peace for all Italians, and that is why this April 18
we are going to vote for the Front. We're going to throw out this government
of clericalists and servants of foreign imperialism that is once
again leading us to ruin. So long, then, until April 18 and victory."
L'Unità [2]

Gino Bartali grabs the yellow jersey!

[1] The Bologna newspaper *Il resto del Carlino* bore the name *Giornale dell'Emilia* (Emilian Daily) between the years 1945 and 1953. During the fascist era in Italy its editorial directorship was in the hands of the regime. In 1945 it was officially purged of fascist influences, but for several years continued to be a right-leaning organ. (Tr.)

[2] The Italian Communist Party's national daily newspaper. (Tr.)

APRIL 14 1948
WEDNESDAY

"INTERVIEW WITH DE GASPARI: TODAY'S CERTAINTIES, TOMORROW'S HOPES." "REVELATIONS CONCERNING ZDANOV'S PLAN TO BRING THE COMMUNISTS TO POWER." "GROWING TENSION IN BERLIN: RUSSIANS THREATEN TO CUT AIR TRANSPORT."

"IN THE NAME OF PEACE, TOGLIATTI CALLS FOR SUSTAINED RESISTANCE TO IMPERIALISM." "THE VATICAN'S SECRET ARCHIVE: READYING TO LEAVE FOR AMERICA." "CGIL[1] BRINGS CONTRADICTIONS IN MARSHALL PLAN TO GOVERNMENT'S ATTENTION."

"BARTALI BEATS COPPI IN THE TUSCAN TOUR."

From the wall a giant Cossack was watching him with a fierce look in his eyes, a bearskin adorned with the red star on his head, and a bayonet between his teeth, one eye deformed by an air bubble trapped beneath the paper. The poster was still wet and shiny with glue and when De Luca brushed against it, stepping to one side to avoid a hole in the sidewalk, it left a sticky silver mark on his trench coat, like a snail's trail.

"Is This Who You're Waiting For?" was written across the poster in snarling italics with broad brushstrokes. De Luca stepped off the sidewalk to take in its entire length. He put his hands in his pockets and pulled his trench coat tight around

---

[1] *Confederazione Generale Italiana del Lavoro* (General Labor Confederation), a communist-led trade union federation founded in 1944. (Tr.)

him. Then he crossed the street, quickening his step suddenly when a jeep came racing out of the gates of the prefecture, then another, and another still, the officers clutching their seats as the jeeps swung out, sirens blaring. De Luca held his breath and watched them go by, his stomach gripped in a clammy stranglehold. He stared after them until they disappeared around the corner of the piazza, and then ran up the stairs of the stationhouse so fast that the guard had to call him twice before he turned, already midway across the lobby floor.

"Hey! Where are you going in such a hurry? Who are you?"

De Luca reached into a pocket to look for his ID card, then the other, then the inside pocket of his trench coat, then he bent forward to search the pockets of his coat.

"First day today," he said. "Special Sub Commissario De Luca, vice squad." But the officer on guard, busy saluting a group of people coming down the stairs, grabbed him by the arm and pulled him brusquely to one side.

"Over here, you . . . let them by."

It was a group of uniformed officers escorting a short, beak-nosed man wearing civvies and a black hat. De Luca, grasping at the guard's arm to avoid falling backwards, thought the man in the hat looked familiar.

"Pugliese!" he cried, and the short man looked up abruptly, as if sniffing the air. He frowned for a second, staring at De Luca, before he recognized him.

"Commissario! What are you doing here in Bologna? Carboni, for fuck's sake, what are you doing? You dare put your hands on a ranking officer?"

The guard pulled his arm away and his hand shot to the brim of his cap so fast that De Luca was left reeling, swaying unsteadily on his heels. Pugliese took his hand, helping him get his balance back.

"I had no idea you were coming here, sir . . . I'm pleased, Commissa! What are you up to? Coming with us?"

De Luca opened his arms wide, hesitant, and threw a glance at the far end of the lobby where a staircase led to the upper floors. "I don't know," he said. "I'm supposed to report to the chief of police . . ."

"The chief is in a meeting with the prefect, about the elections. Come with us, sir . . . There's been a homicide."

De Luca stiffened. He went to follow Pugliese, impulsively, then stopped dead.

"They haven't given me my papers yet," he muttered. "I should probably see the chief first, and, well . . . I'm in vice now . . ."

Already outside, without even turning, Pugliese shrugged.

"Then this concerns you, too," he called. "It happened in a whorehouse."

De Luca bit his lip and shot another glance at the staircase. Then he put his head down, ran outside and jumped aboard the jeep as it pulled out, grabbing hold of an officer's shoulder belt.

"I'm happy that you made it through, Commissa," Pugliese said in his thick Neapolitan accent, clipping the final syllables from De Luca's title.

With one hand holding the collar of his coat closed and the other clutching the roll bar, Pugliese smiled. De Luca watched his eyes carefully, for he thought he noticed a flash, quick as anything, of irony. But Pugliese always had a flash of irony in his eyes, no matter what he said.

"Well, here we are," said De Luca and shrugged.

"How many years has it been, Commissa? Almost three, I'd say . . . No, exactly three. The last time we saw each other was April '45, if I'm not wrong, and here it is April again. Only three years, Commissa, but hard years for someone like you, no? No?"

"Here we are," De Luca repeated. He glanced cautiously,

almost shyly, at the officer sitting next to him and the one sitting up front. But their faces were expressionless, policemen's faces. Faces under orders.

Pugliese leaned forward, gave the driver a slap on the shoulder and pointed to a street.

"We're cutting through town on via Marconi," he explained to De Luca. "It's longer this way but at least we won't get held up in the piazza, with the speeches and all the rest." And then, almost fleetingly, and without that sparkle in his eyes, he said:

"No, really, Commissa . . . I'm happy you made it through."

De Luca nodded, distracted. He had closed his eyes, his hands between his legs clutching the jeep's wooden seat, and it looked as if he were listening to the siren echoing through the porticoed sidewalks. He was leaning slightly forward, like he wanted to hear it better. The wind lifted his hair and sent it flapping against the side of his head. When he opened his eyes he had to blink, repeatedly, in order to clear the mist away.

"Who is it?" he said.

Pugliese looked up.

"Sorry?"

"The victim. You said there'd been a homicide."

"Oh, yeah, the victim. A certain *Ermes* . . . but don't go asking me who this Ermes is, Commissario, because I don't have a clue. Central took the call. The woman was hysterical, screaming 'They've killed Ermes in via delle Oche number 23.' You know what you'll find at via delle Oche number 23?"

De Luca nodded, quickly. "Yes, a whorehouse."

"Sure, easy, all of via delle Oche is one big whorehouse and, oh yeah . . . I already told you. But you'll be learning all about these things on you own, sir, now that you're in vice. Bologna is overflowing with brothels. And now they're all yours, sir."

Once more that flash of irony in Pugliese's eyes, so ironic and so natural that it made De Luca smile. A second later the jeep swerved hard into a narrow street sending De Luca tumbling onto Pugliese, almost as if he wanted to kiss him.

"Number 23 is attached . . . It's not really the cathouse, I mean, no offense to common decency, but . . . how to put it . . . an annex."

The woman was walking quickly up the stairs, holding fast to the banister and stopping every now and again to turn around, mid-step, just for a second, as if she wanted to say something. Then she'd start walking and talking again, turning her enormous buttocks toward De Luca and Pugliese and the two officers behind them. She was wearing a black woolen shawl that had slipped off her shoulders and it was swinging back and forth in time with her hips, making De Luca, closed between the walls of a dark corridor that was as tight as a funnel, feel nauseous. She had run right up to him the minute they turned into the street and introduced herself as the *maîtresse*, dragging out the final "ss"s à la Bolognese, her lips twisting into a mincing grin. Then she turned back to the house and pushed the heads of a handful of girls back inside the doorway, alternately clapping her hands and opening her arms wide like a farmer's wife with a brood of chickens. Only when she had pulled the door closed with a heavy thud and stepped out from under the porticos to glance up at the building's closed shutters did she come back to them, pointing out the white ceramic sign, framed in blue, bearing the number 23, the chipped black door, and the steep stairs running up the dark corridor.

"Because the brothel, no offense, Dottore, is at number 22, but number 23, which is part of the same building that I rent from a signore, and I don't need to tell you who he is because you surely know, number 23, as I was saying, is on the license, but anyway it's not really, as I said, the cathouse . . . no offense."

She had stopped on the landing and was breathing hard, one hand on her breast and the other on her throat, smoothing out the folds of her double chin. She leaned her round shoulders against a light-colored wooden door and looked now at De Luca now at Pugliese, as if trying to decide from whom she was supposed to take orders. Pugliese spoke first.

"Is this it?" he asked, and the woman nodded, firmly. Then she put her hand behind her, placed it flat against the door and pushed it open, without turning.

"If only you knew what a shock it was, Dottore . . ." she began but Pugliese shut her up with an angry gesture. In the middle of the doorway, as if framed by the opening, still and steady as a plumb line suspended above an overturned stool, was a man, hanging from a roof beam by a rope.

"Nobody killed anyone here," whispered Pugliese. "This guy killed himself. The operator at central must have got it wrong . . ."

The woman turned abruptly to face the room. "Oh, God, how horrid!" she cried, covering her eyes as Pugliese leaned out over the banister and called down to the officer that had remained below, telling him to telephone central and let the magistrate know that there's no rush and let the chief of the homicide bureau know that there was no need to come at all.

"Pugliese, come in here for a moment."

De Luca had gone into the room, slipping behind them and through the door, which, having bounced off the wall, was half-closed. When Pugliese came in he found De Luca on the floor beside the overturned stool, looking around the room, pensive: the unmade bed, a bedside table resting on a brick in place of a missing leg, a wicker chair with a coat hanging from the backrest, a cabinet with a row of photographs stuck in its door . . .

"I'd like to ask the signora a question," he said. "Get her in here." Then he stood up, a damp creaking coming from his knees, and swiftly, with the tips of his fingers, slapped the man's hand hanging inert at his side.

"Dear Jesus," groaned the woman as she entered. "What are you doing?"

"Checking rigor mortis. His hand has turned soft again, which suggests that he has been dead since last night, at least. Who was he?" He repeated the words—"Who was he?"— because the woman had glanced apprehensively at Pugliese, who nodded. She decided to answer.

"Ermes Ricciotti. But he doesn't work for me . . . He worked for la Tripolina, four doors down, at number 16. He lived here because Tripolina's place is too small for anyone other than horizontal personnel . . . "

"Horizontal?"

"Yes, that is . . . the whores, if I may . . . without meaning any offense, that is. La Tripolina has got no room for a *man* . . ."

She had pronounced the last word with respect, as if it began with a capital M. When De Luca frowned, she continued, surprised, almost embarrassed by that far too simple explanation. "The man, the seraph, what is it you call him? The one who lends a hand around the place, accompanies the girls, throws the drunks out . . . He was a minder, in short. Ermes was handy with his mitts . . . "

She pointed to a cabinet, to a row of photographs stuck in the crack between the door's ground glass and its wooden frame. De Luca walked over and pulled out one that had fallen over and was hanging by a corner. It was a good photo, an enlargement, with a white border. Ermes Ricciotti was shirtless, his gloved fists held in front of his face. Behind him, the corner post of a boxing ring, and beyond that, in the background, the dark insignia of a gym, Spartaco Community Gym. De Luca turned to look at the hanged man. His nose broken, its point flattened . . . he'd noted it immediately. So, too, the deformed ears, hanging low on either side of a square jaw that was being pushed to one side by the noose. He couldn't have been much more than twenty.

He put the photograph back with the others, all of which were a little older, their corners curled. A bunch of armed men in a Fiat 1100 entering Bologna in front of an American armored car, a kid on the hood who, looking closer at the photo, squinting to focus better, De Luca thought might have been Ricciotti himself. A clipping from a newspaper with a close-up of a girl, her flowing hair blending into the black background, her lips partially closed in a malicious smile, and her chin hidden behind the curve of one bare shoulder, "*La Bella Italiana Competition 1947*" printed diagonally across the photo in fake handwriting. Ricciotti, tiny, out of focus, and yellowed by a stain on the photographic paper as he turns in to via delle Oche astride a Lambretta. One photograph had been removed and only a torn corner remained, a triangle with a white border. There was a light-skinned ankle and a foot shod in a cork-heeled sandal visible in the remnant, and above that, the hem of a striped skirt. De Luca scratched at it with the fingernail of his pinkie finger but the fragment, stuck fast between the wood and the glass, wouldn't budge.

"Go ahead and write Armida," the maîtresse was saying to Pugliese, who had pulled out his notepad. "I mean, my name's Conti Evelina, but they've been calling me Armida since 1920 . . . Anyway, no, I wasn't expecting anything like this. Never seen him as happy as he was in the last few days, poor thing. Ermes . . . one night he even came home drunk, and it wasn't that long ago . . . when did we have the thunderstorm . . . was it Sunday? Yes, then it was the day before yesterday, Monday."

"Are you certain? I don't remember any storm . . ."

"I'm certain, all right . . . The front windows have to stay closed by law but I got the lobby out back and you can see the lightning from there . . . It was Monday."

"Who found him?" De Luca asked. Another second of silence, time enough for the maîtresse to take another quick glance at Pugliese.

"Katy," she said, pronouncing the word with a stress on the *y*. "One of the girls who works down there with us. I sent her up here because Ermes hadn't shown up. You know, Tonino, our man, always gets up late, but Kat*y* is a devotee of the Madonna and so Ermes always took her to say novena in San Petronio on his Vespa. Even if politically speaking," Armida lowered her voice, "politically speaking, I say, Ermes was with the communists. There you have it, I don't know your thoughts on the matter, but there! I told you . . . He was a sympathizer—"

"Take a look around," De Luca cut her short, indicating the room by rotating his hand at the wrist. "Is everything in its place? Is anything different?"

"Answer the commissario," said Pugliese, realizing that De Luca, reacting to the woman's by now predictable silence, had closed his eyes tight and clenched his fists. "He's the commissario, I'm merely a maresciallo. But what are all these questions about, Commissa? What are you looking for?"

"Signs of a struggle."

"Signs of a struggle? But it looks to me like . . . "

Pugliese lifted his hand high, and ran his palm down the length of Ermes's side. De Luca glanced at him, quick, then walked over to Ermes and crouched down, his knees creaking again. He put the stool back on its legs, placing it directly under the toes of the man's shoes, measuring the distance between them and the top of the stool.

"It's normal enough that a hanged man grows a little longer if he's left a while," he murmured. "But I've never heard of one getting shorter."

Pugliese's thin lips curled into an incredulous smile. He ran to the door, stopping for a second at the doorway to turn toward De Luca.

"Christ, Commissario," he said. "I sure am glad you're back!" Then he left the room and yelled down the stairwell for them to call the magistrate and the chief of the homicide bureau, because the kid hadn't killed himself. Somebody had damn well stuck him up there.

"Communist Fanaticism Twice Brings the Riot Squad Into Action." "Father Angelini to the Faithful: Those Against God Cannot Hope for Victories." "Arms Detainer Arrested In Imola."

"Riot Squad Mobilized to Remove Posters." "Whole World Sure of Victory for the Front." "Riot Squad Fires on Crowd in Ostiglia."

"Today at the Fulgor a Bold and Adventurous Film: *Arizona Stagecoach* with Ray Corrigan and John King."

Scelba wants to close the factories from the nineteenth to the twenty-first but the unions don't agree and they won't let him. Better this way, if you ask me . . . better the workers closed up inside than out on the streets when the election results are announced. Whichever way it goes."

Chief of Police Giordano was a short man, almost bald, except for a combover stuck to his head with brilliantine that he was forever slicking down, appearing to suffer from a severe tic. He lifted his arm stiffly, arm and forearm at right angles, his hand hung suspended and cupped at his temple for an instant, and then he ran it quickly over his head, with a sweeping motion that momentarily covered his face. The first few times De Luca had to raise his eyes to the ceiling in order to hide his surprised smile. Nobody else seemed to notice; the other officers in the briefing room didn't stir of the chief's tic. Then, after a few minutes, standing behind the last row of chairs, his arms folded over his chest and his shoulders against the wall, De Luca, like the others, had stopped noticing it.

"The prefect doesn't want any more of the riot squad's armored cars at Porta Lame . . . He says it reminds people of when the Germans were here and comes off like a provocation . . . What is it, D'Ambrogio?"

De Luca turned toward the far corner of the table at which the chief was sitting. A man, extremely tall judging from the long torso shooting up out of the wooden tabletop, was shaking his head, his lips tightly closed and pouting, like a child. His voice, high-pitched, almost a falsetto, made him sound like a little boy.

"I don't think that's such a good idea. It might seem like a sign of weakness on our part, and it's certainly not the moment for that. This morning, at Secchia's campaign speech in piazza Maggiore the social-communists sent five officers to hospital . . ."

"Provocations!" Quickly, the chief swept his hand over his head, holding it steady at the back of his head for a second longer than usual. "Firm hand, always at the ready, but no room for provocations! Send more officers next time . . . What is it, Scala?"

At the other end of the table, a man in a gray double-breasted suit with a white shirt open at the neck had raised his hand, as if he were at school. He smiled, clearly amused.

"Concerning provocations . . ." he said. "What shall we do about Orlandelli? The Civic Committee wants to hold a funeral at San Petronio, with father Lombardi saying Mass . . ."

"Advise against it! Advise against it, in no uncertain terms!" The chief's hand stopped midair and De Luca instinctively held his breath until it moved again, fast, two rapid swipes this time. "Father Lombardi! God's Microphone in Bologna four days shy of the elections? You must be joking? My apologies to the right Honorable, he may well have been born in Strada Maggiore here in Bologna, but he had his heart attack in Rome, and they can take care of his funeral . . . The chief of police is against the idea. End of briefing. Orders remain unchanged for everybody: all bureaus limit their activities to only the most important cases and pull all personnel from what they're doing so that they can be deployed for the elections."

The chief stood up. He gathered the papers that were in front of him and straightened them against the tabletop while mumbling to himself, "End of conversation, end of conversation . . . won't hear of it," and shaking his head at D'Ambrogio, who, leaning over him, seemed even taller. De Luca pushed himself off the wall and made his way through the crowd of officers and bureau chiefs on their way out, pushing against the tide and avoiding, with a sudden movement, falling over a chair directly in front of the chief's table.

"Special Sub Commissario De Luca, Chief, sir," he said, grabbing hold of the seat. "If I may, I would . . ."

"Oh, Dottor De Luca . . . they've told me so many good things about you. Bravo, bravo . . ."

The chief's hand shot up, and De Luca was suckered in. He extended his own hand, at the precise moment that the chief bent his arm at the elbow, and he was left with his hand suspended in midair. He concealed his faux pas by pretending to bat away a fly.

"I'm not a dottore," he said, as if apologizing, "and if I may, sir, concerning your orders to pull personnel from the bureaus . . ."

"Yes, yes, bravo De Luca. Conversation closed, D'Ambrogio, I know Orlandelli was a big shot, loved and respected by one side, but hated with a vengeance by the other . . ."

"And if I may, sir, my office being at full force and with a relatively light workload . . ."

"It would seem like a provocation, D'Ambrogio, I'm surprised at you, of all people, it's not like you're new to the job."

". . . So, if you agree, sir, I could usefully be reassigned to the field operations bureau to take up the case of this morning's homicide."

The chief's eyes narrowed. He looked first at De Luca, then at D'Ambrogio.

"There was a murder this morning?"

"Ermes Ricciotti," De Luca began, in a rush, but D'Ambrogio interrupted him with a high-pitched outburst, two ascending notes, modulated, like a choirboy.

"Suicide . . . Dottor Bonaga, who is in charge of field ops, is convinced that we're dealing with a suicide. The guilty conscience of a dubious character who, furthermore, appears to have been a Communist sympathizer . . ."

"Oh, mercy! If it's a suicide it's a suicide . . . Let's not complicate matters and above all let us give no grist to the mill of political manipulation. Laudable zeal, my dear Dottor De Luca, but stay where you are, at the disposition of your bureau chief. At the Bologna Police Department, my dear De Luca, the blurring of bureaus and their responsibilities is not welcome."

"Not welcome," D'Ambrogio repeated in his high-pitched voice, as the chief raised his arm again and struck De Luca lightly on the cheek, leaving the corner of his mouth twisted into a surprised scowl and his hand still suspended midair, useless.

"*I'm not a dottore, I'm not a dottore* . . ." Scala had come up behind him without De Luca noticing. "I knew another man who was always saying the same thing . . . What was his name . . . Germi, no. Ingravallo . . . Commissario Ingravallo. Do you know him?"

"I ran across him once . . . in Rome."

Scala nodded, wordlessly. He kept staring at him, insistent, with that bemused look in his eyes, as if he might break out in a smile at any moment. De Luca felt the need to speak to fill that cold silence.

"I'm a '28er," he said. "I joined the force when there was the call for enrollees in '28, when there was no need to have a degree to become commissario, the entry exam was enough."

"I was afraid you'd been promoted because of your fascist credentials, back in the days," Scala said. De Luca shook his head.

"No."

"Good for you. How old are you, De Luca? Thirty-seven, thirty-eight . . . under forty, like me? You must have been young in '28."

"I was the youngest commissario in the Italian police force."

"And how'd you do on the entry exam?"

"First place."

Another silence, cold and bemused. Scala had moved over to the door of the room, which in the meantime had emptied out.

"They made me commissario almost immediately," he said, and he said it fast, as if he felt he had to justify himself. "I solved the Matera case, in '29 . . . Perhaps you remember it . . ."

"No," said Scala brusquely, still bemused, but curt. "I was inside in '29. I was one of the clandestine leaders of the Italian Communist Party and I was young, too, very young, when they arrested me at the border with France. A tipoff. I was returning to Italy with a case full of documents, but instead of comrades there waiting for me, I found Mussolini's policemen. Naturally . . ." Scala eyes flashed on those of De Luca, who moved uneasily amidst the empty chairs, "naturally, you came out of the purge clean . . . Naturally."

"Naturally," mumbled De Luca. He was expecting that very question and he had even swallowed to clear his throat so he could answer clearly. Nonetheless, his voice came out thick and a little wavering. Scala smiled, this time with his mouth as well as his eyes.

"It's a shame that talent like yours is being wasted in brothels. You should be in the homicide bureau, in place of that

Bonaga . . . Good fellow, God knows, but limited, with a ten-
dency to close cases in a hurry, especially when they involve
comrades. But if you ask me, we've got ourselves an interesting
case in this Ricciotti affair . . . Don't you think?" He squeezed
De Luca's arm, pulling himself away from the door and repeated himself: "Don't you think?" He was bemused, Scala, forever
bemused.

"Let's pretend we're at school, Maresciallo. Give me a history lesson."

Pugliese lifted his nose up from the tabletop and for a
moment he looked at De Luca with the same surprised expression that President De Nicola had in the photo hanging on the
wall behind Pugliese's head. Two pairs of eyes, wide open, suspicious and disoriented, stared at him as he stood in the doorway, one hand on his hip and the other on the doorjamb, narrow and rectangular like the office itself.

"Sorry?" Pugliese said.

De Nicola didn't say a word.

"Teach me a little bit of history, Maresciallo, just to get
things straight . . . How is it that in half a day a suicide becomes
a homicide and then becomes a suicide again?"

"Dottor Bonaga, my boss and the man responsible for the
case, read the report and declared himself convinced that it
was *a case of intentional suicide.*"

"Intentional suicide? Is that what he said?"

Pugliese nodded, slowly, his head leaning slightly to one
side as if to give greater solemnity to his gesture.

"His precise words. I quote: 'A case of intentional suicide.'"

"Oh yeah? And how does he explain it? What does Dottor
Bonaga say, that Ricciotti got up on the stool and, realizing
he'd tied the noose too high, he leapt up and threw his head
into the noose and he . . ." De Luca stopped, because Pugliese
had looked away and his gaze had slipped down onto the desk,

embarrassed, finding nothing there that was dignified enough to stop its course. "Come off it, Pugliese! Impossible! Is that really what he said?"

"He didn't say it, Commissa . . . He wrote it. It's all here in the report he signed and that I've just countersigned, as per regulations . . . God damn that stiff!"

He pushed the document away from him, brusquely, with his fingers, a movement that was almost a slap, sending it sliding off the end of the desk. It planed lightly over to De Luca's feet, like a paper airplane. De Luca looked down at the sheet of carbon copy lying across the toe of his shoe, the black typewritten lines that had punched holes in the thin paper and the smudged words *Bologna Police Department* stamped in a corner. Then he raised his eyes, because Pugliese had stood up, scraping the legs of his chair across the floor. He slipped between the desk and the protruding handles of a file cabinet. President De Nicola, whose black frame Pugliese had brushed against as he passed, swayed back and forth.

"Let's go get a coffee, Commissario," Pugliese said, taking his hat off a coat rack nailed to the wall. "That way I can also give you a lesson on geopolitics." Then he said, "No, no, leave it there, that's the right place for it," because De Luca had just bent down to pick up the sheet of paper. He froze at Pugliese's words, the tip of his middle finger brushing against the smooth surface of the paper, and Pugliese took him by the elbow.

"Do you remember the name they had for it during the days of the regime? Geopolitics . . . No, *Ggeoppollittics*, with every consonant rolled and doubled for the right effect, as Starace used to say. Do you remember Starace?"[1]

---

[1] Achille Starace (1889-1945), secretary of the National Fascist Party, famous for his adherence to and insistence on "fascist modes" of behaving and speaking. (Tr.)

De Luca nodded impatiently. His elbows on the counter of the bar, he was looking at his reflection in the chrome of the coffee machine, a *Vittoria* as imposing as the boiler of a locomotive. Beneath an eagle that had been polished to perfection, perched on a cupola, a barman in a white shirt was twisting the handle of a portafilter, sealing in the pungent, bitter and slightly metallic aroma of the coffee. The bar was in piazza Galileo, right in front of the stationhouse; but nobody ever went there, Pugliese explained. No cops anyway, because there was nowhere to sit. There was only one small table, with no chairs, wedged in between one side of the double door, the edge of the wall, and a large photograph of Bartali.

"There's also Maldini's, next door, they've always got fresh cornetti," whispered Pugliese, covering his mouth with his hand. "But it's like the field ops bureau in there, full of cops, and if you've got to talk Bologna Police Department geopolitics you're better off staying in the station. You remember what they used to say during the days of the regime? 'Silence, the enemy is listening . . . even the walls have ears . . .'"

De Luca nodded again, as his nose, deformed in the coffee machine's chrome plating, grew long and then short, like a mask. The mention of fresh cornetti made him look at the wicker basket on the counter behind Pugliese. He remembered that he hadn't eaten and he reached out to take one, with his bare hand, without picking up one of the squares of baker's paper piled next to the basket.

"Buon appetito, Commissa," Pugliese said. "When I left you, you didn't eat and you didn't sleep, ever . . . You were as pale as a corpse, and thin. Blame it on your worries . . . You don't have all those worries anymore, no?"

"No worries anymore, sure . . ." muttered De Luca.

"And I remember you were already commissario in the FO bureau in '45, and now you're a sub commissario, safeguarding public morals, in vice . . ."

"That's life."

" . . . But you'll always be a commissario as far as I'm concerned, Commissa, hell, you know that, don't you? You used to drink a load of coffee . . . Now too?"

"Now too."

"Even the trench coat looks to be the same one you had back then . . . Similar, more or less . . ."

"More or less."

"But you don't wear the black shirt anymore."

"Maresciallo Pugliese . . . That's enough!"

He had whispered, an almost voiceless whisper, but it was a resonant, sonorous whisper that made even the barman turn. De Luca lowered his eyes, blushing, and stared at the burnt corner of the cornetto he was squeezing between his fingers, nervously.

"Sorry, Commissario, sir," Pugliese mumbled. "Let's get back to department geopolitics," and he pronounced the word "geopolitics" without Starace's double consonants. "That way you can get a handle on the situation and decide how to behave. Dottor D'Ambrogio, the chief's vicar, is on the side of the Christian Democrats . . . No party membership card, of course, because you know it's not allowed on the force, but he's the CD's man. He's a friend of that young undersecretary down in Rome, that short fellow, hunchbacked, ears sticking out . . . I don't remember his name anymore, I'm sorry."

De Luca shrugged. The smell of hot coffee wafted out from the Vittoria, making him swallow. He was listening to Pugliese, rapt, but he couldn't tear his eyes from the bubbling dark rivulet that had begun to flow into the white cup.

"The department's cabinet chief, Dottor Scala, is with the Italian Communist Party. He's one of the few partisan police officers that Scelba hasn't yet ousted, but he's got his ass covered in Rome, too, and he's also a friend of Mayor Dozza here in Bologna. The chief of police, on the other hand, is a nobody, he just wants to hold on to his job, avoid everything that's even remotely political, and wait to see who wins the elections . . . Like all of us."

"And Bonaga?"

"Bonaga's an idiot. He does what they tell him to do, whoever does the telling. If nobody says anything, he does nothing and tries to keep out of the way."

"And who told him to close the case? D'Ambrogio?"

"Who knows? A suicide he says! He may even have had that stroke of genius all by himself. He's where he is because he's a daddy's boy, insofar as his father is the prefect in Trapani, but as soon as they find someone better they'll throw him out and put somebody else in charge of field ops. If you don't do anything crazy, there's a good chance they'll give the job to you, Commissario. If you don't do anything crazy."

De Luca pressed his lips closed, then opened them again suddenly, cutting off an anxious sigh that stuck in his throat. He lifted his hand, a quick movement like he was shooing something away, and shook his head.

"All right, all right . . ." he mumbled. The coffee had arrived with a crisp *tink* of the cup being set on its saucer. De Luca nodded at Pugliese, who was holding a teaspoon of sugar suspended above his cup and nodded again, twice. He drank without stirring the sugar, removing the cup from his mouth when the grains of sugar met his lips.

If you don't do anything crazy. If you don't do anything crazy.

"Pugliese, I'm curious by nature and I don't like unsolved whodunits. I don't know about you, but this gentleman who performed acrobatic feats to get his head in a noose annoys me, almost in a physical way, and I just know that I'm not going to be able to sleep at night. Tell me, Pugliese, in your opinion would I be doing something crazy if I went to see this Tripolina and asked a few questions about Ricciotti?"

Pugliese smiled, mischievously, and glanced sideways at De

Luca, who was staring at the empty coffee cup like he wanted
to read his fortune in the coffee grounds.

"It would be for me, yes, because my boss has closed the
case. I countersigned it, for Christ's sake, and now it's no
longer a matter for my office. But for you, a vice officer . . . asking some questions about this kid who worked as a minder in
a brothel and who happened to kill himself ain't all that
strange." He glanced at De Luca again, quickly, deviously,
almost smiling. "It's not like we're talking about opening up an
investigation, no? Just a few questions."

"Just a few questions," De Luca repeated.

"To make things a little clearer . . ."

"A little clearer, sure . . ."

They stood up from the counter at the same time but
Pugliese beat him to the punch; he put his thumb to his index
finger and with a flourish charged the bill to his account before
De Luca could so much as touch his wallet.

"SIGNORE AND SIGNORINE PLEASE NOTE: BE SURE TO FOLD THE BALLOT WITHOUT SMEARING IT WITH LIPSTICK. IT IS ABSOLUTELY FORBIDDEN TO MAKE ANY SUPERFLUOUS MARKS, SIGN THE BALLOT, AND TO WRITE 'HURRAY' OR 'DOWN WITH.' THE PENCIL MUST BE RETURNED TO PERSONNEL."

Held in place by radiating metal spokes, yellowed by years of use and the incandescent lights, the glass lunettes over the doors on via delle Oche looked like lemon wedges. Bitter lemons, pale, for though the gray light of evening was fast encroaching it was still not dark enough to turn on the lights and the light bulbs behind the ground glass looked dull in the setting sun.

There were already a few people out on the street. A man beneath the porticos, walking fast, glued to the wall, his hat pulled down over his eyes; another in front of a door, one foot on the step and his hand on the wall next to the doorbell, drumming his fingers; two soldiers, in the middle of the street. Only one of them was in uniform, but the other one might just as well have been wearing his too; young, short buzz cut highlighting his round head, and already drunk, jumping in and out of the thin rivulet of water running down the drain in the middle of the road.

"Bologna is a red town, all right," said Pugliese, touching De Luca on the elbow with his fingertips. He lifted his chin with a sudden jerk, like some kind of predator, and gestured toward a poster attached to one of the portico columns facing the street. It was too large for the column and the two sides had been folded back over the corners of the column transforming it into a white square. But it was clear it was a funeral notice; black border framing large block letters, "The Right Honorable Goffredo Orlandelli," and under that in narrow italics, "Kt. Comm. Att. Dr."

"Plastering the Right Honorable Home and Church's funeral announcement on a column in via delle Oche almost smacks of blasphemy."

De Luca smiled and pointed to another sign propped up against a closed window, virtually behind the same column. "You'll find *la Ferrarese* here," it said, in uneven block letters written in red pencil.

"Maybe that one's more suitable," he said. Then he pointed in the same direction but this time at a house number stamped on a white tile, right between the poster leaning up against the window and the closed double door. It was number 16 all right, but the lunette over the door, rectangular and covered by the close-set radiating bars of a grate, wasn't lit.

"There isn't even a doorbell," said Pugliese. He hammered on the door with his closed fist, twice. He got a thin splinter stuck under the skin on the side of his hand for his troubles.

"Damn it," grumbled Pugliese, glancing sideways at a man in a short jacket cut from an old military topcoat who had joined the queue and was grinning at him. De Luca came over to the door and he was about to knock as well when a window covered by a grate in the wall beneath them, low to the ground like basement window, opened and a thin voice, almost like a child's, spoke.

"We're closed . . . Who is it?"

De Luca leaned down to the grate, his hands on his knees.

"Sub Commissario De Luca," he said. "Vice squad."

The man in the short jacket quit smiling, saluted them with a swift movement of his head and left in a hurry. Inside the house, too, somebody had moved back fast. There had been a quick shuffling of slippers behind the door, a rustling of fabric that had become a damp slapping sound, as if the child had taken off her shoes to run faster. De Luca sighed, looked at Pugliese, who was sucking the side of his hand, and then raised his arm. But he didn't manage to knock this time either. There was another shuffle, clearer and less hesitant, coming toward the door, then a moment of silence, an ever so slight hesitation, followed by the dry retort of the door opening, almost as if it had been torn from its frame. A strong pungent odor assailed De Luca, making him screw up his eyes and gulp down the acidic taste of lemon, his lips disfigured in a pained grimace.

"It's Lysol," said the woman. "We're closed and we're doing the cleaning."

"You do the cleaning at night?" Pugliese asked. He had stepped back beneath the portico.

"New girls haven't arrived yet. In the meantime . . ."

"And you want to poison yourselves to death, just to get the cleaning done?"

"It's worse here because we're not allowed to open the front windows, by law. And, anyway, we're used to it."

De Luca coughed into his closed fist, one sharp bark that cleared his throat and brought tears to his eyes. For a moment the woman in front of him seemed covered by a thin shiny veil, making him think of those close-ups you see of American actresses, softened by filters like they were part of a mirage. He stood asking himself the reason why such a thought would come to his mind. The woman must have noticed the look in his eyes, because she stared back at him, suspicious. She didn't really resemble an American actress at all. She was too slovenly, too chunky, too worn, and too dark. Her hair was black, tied in a bun at the back of her head, with one long wavy lock that fell onto her shoulders and another, not as wavy, that fell over her brow, curled like an arch, almost reaching into her eyes.

Her eyebrows had been penciled, black and straight like the wrinkles that lined her high cheekbones and the corners of her full mouth. Her lips were extraordinarily dark. She could have been around thirty, and she wasn't pretty.

"The signora is offending common decency," said Pugliese, mischievously, and it was only then that De Luca realized that the woman was wearing a light-colored negligee that only just covered her knees and a woolen shawl, also black, over her shoulders.

"This is my house," said the woman, still staring at De Luca. "And we're closed."

Pugliese smiled, with a snort that sounded something like a growl.

"I been on the force twenty years and I've never seen a maîtresse leave a commissario from the vice squad standing on the doorstep."

"I don't leave anybody standing on the doorstep. *Public Safety officials are entitled to enter houses of assignation at any moment.* You're the ones standing in the doorway. If you want, come right on in."

She didn't move. De Luca stretched his neck and glanced over her shoulder at the foyer paved with dirty white tiles that reached halfway up the wall, at the table on which stood a lamp crowned by a crooked lampshade with torn tassels, at the staircase in the back and the metal banister disappearing into the darkness. It looked more like a public toilet than a brothel.

"No matter," he said, stopping Pugliese who had moved a step forward as if he was about to push the woman aside and storm in. "We only want to ask a few questions, just to close the case. Ermes Ricciotti . . ."

"He's dead."

"Yes, we know. Ermes Ricciotti . . ."

"He hung himself."

De Luca nodded, cutting short a sigh that was stinging his throat with the taste of Lysol.

"We know that too. We know a whole bunch of things and we'd like to know some more. You're la Tripolina, right? What is your name Signora Tripolina?"

"Claudia."

"And then? Claudia Tripolina?"

"No, Tagliaferri Caludia. Tripolina is a *nom d'arte*."

"Good . . . well then, Signora Tagliaferri Claudia, nom d'arte Tripolina, now you can tell me what kind of character this Ricciotti was, who he spent his time with and why, in your opinion, he killed himself . . . Then, you can let me speak with the girls Ricciotti knew best. If you don't cooperate, I'm going back to the station to read up on Article 7 of the Public Safety Act, the one about prostitution, and you'll see, I'll find a way to pull your license, Signora Tagliaferri Claudia, nom d'arte Tripolina."

"Signorina."

De Luca clenched his jaw as a chill ran up his spine. He glanced at Pugliese, who was smiling incredulously, his mouth agape, and then turned back to the woman, who was still staring at him, straight in the eyes, her arms hanging down over her satin hips and her lips closed tight, marked in the middle by a line that was growing whiter and whiter. There was something in her look, Tagliaferri Claudia, nom d'arte Tripolina, not signora but signorina, standing there without moving a muscle, framed by the doorway of a brothel that seemed more like a public piss house, something in her look halfway between rage and fear. For a second, only a second, it looked more like fear than rage, then Tagliaferri Claudia, nom d'arte Tripolina, signorina and not signora, bent down, quickly, removed a slipper from one foot and, with a swift wallop that echoed through the foyer, flattened a cockroach that was climbing the wall.

"Madonna mia!" cried Pugliese. He had jumped at the

sound. "Commissario, I'm going next door to call the office and see if they've been looking for me . . . That way at least I'll be able to settle down some. If I may, let me give you a tip for the arrest: that voice we heard before at the door belonged to a minor and perhaps the Signorina Tripolina is unaware that in houses of assignation minors under the age of eighteen are not allowed. If I may."

"Lisetta is no minor . . . She's eighteen, even if she does have the voice of a child. I know the law."

She spoke quietly, firmly but without raising her voice, almost as if talking to herself. She had stopped staring at De Luca, the slipper still in her hand and her one bare foot wedged against her knee. Her negligee had slid back on her leg and De Luca noticed that she wasn't as chunky and round as she first seemed. And her face, too, wasn't all that drawn . . . weathered, yes, but not entirely. She may have been thirty, and who knows, perhaps she was even pretty.

"Were you really born in Tripoli?" he asked. La Tripolina shook her head. She cleaned the toe of her slipper against the doorjamb and dropped it on the ground, turning it over with her foot and pushing against the door in order to slip it on.

"No, I was born in Alexandria. But not Alexandria in Egypt . . . Alexandria in Piedmont. They call me Tripolina because I worked in the colonies, for two years, during the war. They called me that before as well, because my skin has always been dark . . ."

"What was Ricciotti like?"

La Tripolina raised her eyes, again with that hard look in them. She pressed her lips together. De Luca closed his eyes and his jaw muscles tightened. His voice came out between his teeth in a whisper.

"Tomorrow morning at the station. You and all the girls who knew Ricciotti . . ." he said, hitting the poster leaning up against the window with every syllable, "including la Ferrarese here."

La Tripolina opened her lips, holding back a sigh that was almost a sob, again surprising De Luca and making him frown. She leaned out the door, closing her negligee across her bosom and pulled the sign out of the window, then she looked up because the shutters of the house across the street opened with a piercing screech caused by years of rust. De Luca also turned. They both looked up at Pugliese, who was holding the window open with two hands. Behind him a woman was trying to close them, repeating, "Dottore, it's not allowed, Dottore."

"Commissa, I got to get back," Pugliese yelled. "And I'm asking you this as a personal favor, come with me . . . They've cut some guy's throat, in Montagnola."

"Printer's Shop Destroyed in Reggio: An Issue of *Penna* with Revelations about the K Plan Ruined."

"Silence on Monarchist-Fascist Arms Trafficking in Bologna."

The grass shone under the photographers' flashbulbs. Lit up for a split second it appeared sharp, each blade visible, red and slick, then became an indistinct patch once more, darker than the rest of the lawn that dropped away sharply and disappeared amidst the hills of Montagnola park. In the middle of the patch, his legs lying uphill and crossed like the number four and his hands over his head pointing down hill, was a man, he too illuminated by the cameras' flashbulbs that reflected furiously against the metal buttons of his coat, against his glasses sitting diagonally across his brow, and even against his teeth, bared, his mouth open in a twisted smile.

"No way you can say this was a suicide, Commissa . . . Watch out for the bicycle."

A bicycle with solid rubber tires was lying on its side along the path at the top of the drainage ditch and De Luca lifted one leg, stepping over it, almost without thinking. He was enthralled by the scene. He stared down at the cadaver in the middle of the dark patch, at the uniformed officers guarding it, at the police photographers. He would have started running to get down there faster, but the descent was steep and dark, lit only by a night watchman's carbide lamp. Then a Fiat 1100 shot out from between the trees and stopped at the top of the hill with its motor running. A uniformed officer got out with a cable clamp in his hands and opened the trunk. Blinding and sudden, like that of the flashbulbs, the white beam of a spotlight carried De Luca's shadow over the grass. It came to rest on the cadaver in the middle of the bloodied grass.

A man with a trench coat over his shoulders got out of the 1100. He ran and slipped down the little ditch as he passed by De Luca, who helped him up by the arm. De Luca noted that beneath the trench coat the man was wearing a tuxedo with a white bow tie.

"What the hell is going on?" yelled the man, coming to a stop one step from the cadaver. He lifted his foot to scrutinize his patent leather shoes in the spotlight's beam, groaning, "Oh God, this is blood!" and quickly jumped back out of the patch of dark grass. "Pugliese," he cried, wiping the sole of his shoe on the ground. "Maresciallo Pugliese! What the fuck is going on here?"

"One dead, Dottore," Pugliese said with a sigh. "Murdered. Stand over there on the gravel, otherwise you'll get your clothes wet . . . "

De Luca had come nearer. His hands were in his pockets lifting up the cuffs of his trousers as he stood next to the night watchman who was holding the carbide lamp. He put his hand on the man's arm and lowered the lamp to better see the corpse's face. A man in shirtsleeves kneeling down beside the cadaver raised his thumb approvingly.

"Right, that's the way . . . thanks. A little further down. I'd like to see his hands. He must have scratched like a damn cat, all his fingernails are broken . . . "

"Is that gold?" asked De Luca, pointing at a necklace that had caught the light.

"It's gold all right. On his fingers as well . . . a ring as big as this. And his watch."

"Wallet?"

"Here it is, Dottore . . . "

A uniformed officer leaned across the night watchman and handed De Luca a thin wallet made of pale leather. The officer pulled his arm back immediately because he was blocking the light and the man in shirtsleeves was already getting his lips around some vulgarity or another. De Luca held the wallet in the palm of his hand, as if weighing it: light, thin and smooth with a flower embroidered in the leather. A dandy's wallet, refined, almost feminine. He was about to open it when the man in the tuxedo came over to him, walking on tiptoes.

"Commissario Bonaga, chief of homicide," he said. He extended his hand and De Luca looked at it for a moment because he thought the man wanted to shake hands, but his palm was facing upwards.

"Ah, of course . . . " said De Luca, "the wallet." He placed it on the man's fingers, turning red, without really knowing whether it was embarrassment or anger that made him blush. Bonaga repeated De Luca's movements, holding the wallet in the palm of his hand, and then gave it to Pugliese.

"This is all we need," he said. "Between you and me . . . You see how I'm dressed? Just think, my fiancée and I were on our way to see Totò's latest revue, 'Be Careful I Don't Eat You,' when they called me from the station . . . I mean, *at home*. Can you believe it?"

He put a hand on his shoulder, jocular, but De Luca didn't notice. He was looking at Pugliese, stretching his neck to see what was in the wallet.

"Piras Osvaldo, son of Gavino, deceased, born in Sassari in 1902 . . . " said Pugliese, turning the ID card to catch the light.

"But, it's not so bad here, you'll see. It's a quiet town, except for the occasional incident, like this here . . . "

Pugliese took a few folded one-hundred-lire bills from the wallet and counted them out quickly between his thumbs.

"Three," he murmured, glancing at De Luca. Then he slipped his fingers into one of the wallet's compartments, pulled out a piece of paper folded in four and opened it.

"And the chief of police is a reasonable man, that is, if he's still around after the elections, of course . . . "

Pugliese looked at De Luca, who was shrugging, trying his best to look disinterested. But he couldn't resist.

"What is it?" he asked

"Right, what is it?" asked Bonaga, distracted. Pugliese lifted up the piece of paper and held it open with three fingers so that De Luca could see it.

"A flier. Photography studio on via Marconi. Our man Piras was a photographer."

Bonaga raised his hand and flapped it around in front of his face, as if swatting the words away.

"Fine, Maresciallo, fine. Gather everything up and we'll look at it tomorrow morning, at the station. Everything seems pretty clear, no? This fellow was riding through the park on his way home and they killed him for money . . . "

"He's still got his money on him, Dottore," mumbled Pugliese, with a mischievous smile. He looked at De Luca, who was holding his chin and staring at the grass, thoughtful.

"Well, then, a whoremonger!" said Bonaga. "They work around here, don't they? He's even half naked! It's clear as day: he and his worldly companion were looking for a quiet spot . . . "

"I was thinking the same thing," said De Luca, to himself. "But we'd have found his bicycle leaning up against a tree and not at the top of the drainage ditch. They stopped him for a reason, they cut his throat in the middle of the road and he fell down the slope here. Then they started rifling through his pockets but the night watchman arrived and they took off."

Bonaga put his hand on De Luca's shoulder again and this

time he felt it, heavy and annoying, like the smell of brilliantine that wafted over, strong, even in the open air, when Bonaga leaned his head toward De Luca.

"Whoa there, colleague . . . Go easy with the theories. Until proven otherwise I'm the chief of homicide and I don't want you—"

"But look, look . . . "

Pugliese had been fishing around in the wallet. He pushed a square card out of one of the wallet's pockets.

"This one's a communist, Commissa. He's even got a party membership card."

Bonaga jumped forward, forgetting about his fancy shoes as they sunk into the bloodied grass, and snatched the wallet out of Pugliese's hands.

"A communist? Now you tell me! Give me that."

He slipped the card completely out of the wallet and ran back toward the rise, leaning forward, one hand almost touching the ground to stop himself from slipping over.

"In your opinion, who's he going to call? Scala or D'Ambrogio?" asked Pugliese.

"Maybe both. Though the logical thing to do would be to go straight to the deceased's home. If they didn't kill him for money, either they already found what they were looking for because he carried it on his person, or they came up empty-handed because he kept whatever it was at home."

"Christ, Commissa . . . You need a court order to search an apartment."

"Sure. But not to inform family members, if there are any, of the death, and taking a little look around while we're there wouldn't be that difficult."

"And if he doesn't have any family members living with him? If he lived alone?"

"Then we'll get the doorman to open the apartment."

Pugliese sighed, shrugging.

"I don't know, I don't know . . . Commissa, I'm in the homicide bureau and I get my orders from dottor Bonaga . . . "

"And I'm in vice, and I get my orders from myself. Give me the deceased's address, Maresciallo, and I'll take care of the uncomfortable task of alerting family members for you."

Pugliese shook his head and bit his lip. Then he threw his arms open and let them fall back against his legs with a loud slap.

"A building in via Marconi . . . But I'm not telling you which, I'm coming with you. Christ, Commissa, when Bonaga comes back and doesn't find me here, he's going to want my balls . . . "

"You make out like everything's easy, but even doing things like this we should have a search warrant . . . "

De Luca touched his nose with the tip of his finger and Pugliese nodded, raising one hand. He had whispered because the doorman had his back to them but he was still near enough to hear. Then he disappeared behind the curtain of his lodgings. He returned carrying a ring of keys so full that it didn't even rattle when he tossed it from one hand to the other as he stood in front of his office scratching his head above a few strands of hair that he had combed over his pate.

"But listen here, Commissario, it doesn't seem right going up there in this fashion. . . Did they really kill signor Piras?"

He shrugged when De Luca nodded and came out from the doorman's room gesturing toward the elevator cage with his chin. "Okay then . . . I don't reckon anybody'll be objecting. He was always alone, was Signor Piras . . . except for his *visitor*." He turned back to look over his shoulder when he spoke these last words, sliding open the iron gate of the elevator cage. And he repeated himself as he opened the two halves of the double doors and entered, his lips pulled back over his teeth, his voice coming out in a thin hiss. "Strange little lady, friendly . . . You understand what I mean?"

"We understand, all right," said Pugliese, getting in the elevator. "Bonaga might have been right, Commissa. There's always a first time . . . "

The porter stood aside to let De Luca pass, and then he leaned out of the elevator and pushed on a light switch on the wall in front of them. The timer jumped to life and the high oval staircase at the center of the building was illuminated.

"Certain things never used to happen," he said, slapping his hand against the dark marble banister that curled around the elevator. "Say what you want . . . say he was a scoundrel, even a delinquent, but when he was around certain things never happened! There you go . . . and now, if you want, you can slap the cuffs on me!"

The doorman held his arms out, his wrists crossed and his fists closed. He lifted his chin and a few strands of his comb-over fell down on his forehead. The buzz of the timer died and all of a sudden the entire stairwell went dark. De Luca, leaning against the mirror at the back of the elevator, snorted, annoyed, crossing his arms over his chest.

"Let's get a move on, if you don't mind."

"Right," said Pugliese. "Don't worry about the timer and in you get. We'll head up in the dark. And keep your political comments to yourself. Anyway, in a few days, we'll be voting."

"Oh yes . . . and you can count on me giving my vote to the Uomo Qualunque[1]! We were better off when we were worse off, I'm telling you . . . "

The porter pushed the button for the top floor and the metal cage left the ground with a jerk. Pugliese didn't respond, but even in the dark De Luca could tell he was smiling. He, on the other hand, sighed, immersed in the almost total darkness, ascending, accompanied by the ever so slight vibration of the

---

[1] The Uomo Qualunque Front (Common Man Front) was a conservative political party founded in 1944 and dissolved in 1948. (Tr.)

elevator, moving so slowly it hardly seemed as if they were moving at all. His eyes were beginning to adjust to the darkness. He could almost make out the white painted walls passing before him. It bothered him, and he closed his eyes. He was weary. He could feel exhaustion assailing him from behind, as always, a sensation that was almost physical weighing on the back of his head and his shoulders, making him unfold his arms and hang them loosely at his side. In his head, in his mind, random words pertaining to Piras and Montagnola and all the possible developments in the case kept twisting themselves together. But despite the medley of words, he could easily have lowered his chin on his chest, right there and then, and fallen into a fitful sleep. If it weren't for Pugliese. His voice carried a touch of anxiety as it came out through his lips, making De Luca open his eyes suddenly.

"There's a light on up there."

De Luca looked up at the black line of the landing descending slowly toward them and noticed a thin yellow strip of light shining under the door. He had only just made out the darker patches that interrupted the strip of light and continued upwards, well-defined like the shape of a man standing against the light, when he saw the flames, long and bluish, and the sparks shooting off the metal gate, flashing bright red in the darkness.

The porter cried out and so did De Luca, curled up in the corner of the elevator, crushed more by the deafening sound of the gunfire than by fear. He reached into the pocket of his trench coat to search for his pistol, but Pugliese had already pulled his out and had started firing, two, three, four shots that filled the tiny space with a storm of splintered wood and glass. The shots echoed in his stomach, making it impossible to breathe, and when the elevator lurched to a stop De Luca threw himself against the wobbly panels of the elevator door, guided by the sound of broken glass, his fingers struggling frantically with the gate latch.

Somebody turned the lights on. De Luca found himself on the landing, bent at the knees, his arms open and his pistol in one hand, dazed and immobile as if he were posing for a photograph. Pugliese was standing in the same position looking at him. One door on the landing was wide open and they ran toward it, bursting into the apartment.

"Fuck's sake!" Pugliese cried, slipping face first down on the floor. De Luca jumped over an overturned chair and only avoided tripping on a drawer that had been pulled out of its dresser by steadying himself quickly against the corner of a table. It looked like a bomb had exploded inside, covering the floor with papers, books and broken glass, and the sofa had been torn open with a knife and its innards scattered. There was an open window in front of him and he ran in that direction, holding fast to the sill and leaning out just in time to see a man, stooped, running across the roof, hopping over the barrel tiles. He put one leg out, the tip of his shoe touching the tiles that sloped downwards toward the street below. But something gripped his stomach when he looked over the gutter. He stopped, raised his pistol, closed his left eye and aimed, bringing the shadow, a stooped form silhouetted against an ashen moon partially covered by a cobalt cloud, into his sights. He yelled, "Police! Stop or I'll shoot!"

The shadow halted, making itself smaller, and for a brief second turned its face to the side, giving De Luca a fleeting glimpse of its profile, lit by the blue light. Then it shot to the side, galloping frantically across the roof. There was a clip-clop of heels on the tiles as the man sprinted toward the building across the street. And for a moment it looked like he really was flying, his arms above his head, his legs pulled back like a bird and his trench coat open and flapping in the air like wings. But the illusion only lasted a second. Then De Luca heard the thud, and the sound of fingernails scratching futilely at the wall. The shadow screamed, falling fast like a stone in a sack—

a scream followed by a dull definitive thud that made De Luca pull his head in between his shoulders.

"Pugliese! Maresciallo Pugliese, get up here!"

Leaning over the stairwell, his hands on the black banister to assuage the light sense of vertigo that afflicted him every time he looked down from some high place, De Luca could hardly hear his own voice. The five flights of stairs, coiling upwards, were full of people, in dressing gowns, in pajamas, in civilian clothes and in uniform, all of them getting louder and louder. There was a buzz that became a murmur, then a hub-bub, then an indistinct holler echoing between the landings, winding its way into the apartments, rising up through the soul of the building, filling it with a racket that was so intense and solid that it could almost be touched.

The residents of the building had come out at the first shots, as if they had been waiting behind their doors. And they'd gotten in Pugliese's way as he ran down the stairs, against the current. A man in a dressing gown, seeing him running with pistol in hand, had even gone so far as to claw at the collar of his coat crying, "What have you done, you scoundrel?" De Luca had put his gun back in his pocket and his hands up in front of his chest, stationing himself at the doorway to the apartment, repeating the words "Police! No entry, police!" Pushing the residents back, he finally managed to clear the landing of people. Then he had wedged a chair up against the doorway and kneeled down on the floor, amidst the scattered papers and the overturned drawers, rummaging, more with his hands than his eyes. That's how the first FOB officer found him. Running in, he knocked his shin against the overturned chair and growled, "Fuck's sake!" like Pugliese, then put his hand on his pistol, still resting in his shoulder holster. A woman stopped him. She was dressed in a nightgown and had a coat that she had cut from a German topcoat clasped to her breast. She put a hand on the officer's arm and whispered, "Leave him alone, he's a police officer," in a tone that was both peremptory and maternal. Perhaps because of the tone, or perhaps because of the shadow of the German MP stripes on the topcoat, the officer nodded and brought his hand to the visor of his cap when De Luca brusquely pushed him aside and ran to the banister.

"Maresciallo Pugliese! Come here, I've found something!"

When De Luca heard the metallic grind of the elevator he went back inside Piras's apartment. He sat on the edge of the sofa on a red cushion that had been split in two by a slash as large as a gape-mouthed smile and cleared a space on the glass table in front of him. He placed the shell of a camera on the table and looked at it. The camera's back had been torn off, and the take-up spool was bent. De Luca had found it on the ground, behind a black curtain that separated the room from the photography studio. He found the photographs he was holding, on the other hand, behind a chest of drawers, all doubled up and scattered, as if they had fallen there accidentally. One was larger than the others. It had a white border. In one corner the words, "Ermes and Lisetta, soon to be married," had been written by hand. Beneath the words there was a minute girl, very young, embracing Ermes Ricciotti—he, rigid, in a coat and tie, while she, Lisetta, seemed more relaxed, dressed in a striped skirt and cork-heeled sandals, the same sandals and the same skirt that appeared in the torn corner of the photograph that he had found stuck in the cabinet in Ermes' apartment. They were smiling, papier-mâché ocean waves in the background, a piece of which De Luca had found behind the black curtain. The strange fact was that Ermes Ricciotti appeared in all of the other photographs as well. Each and every one of them with a white border, and in each and every one, Ermes Ricciotti, wearing coat and tie, stiff. Only the girl changed, and the name: *Assuntina, Teresina, Lisetta . . .*

"Perhaps I didn't explain myself clearly enough, Dottor De Luca."

De Luca looked up and saw not Pugliese standing in the doorway but D'Ambrogio. It took a few seconds to recognize him because heaving that voice he had turned expecting to see a child and not a man, certainly not a man as tall as D'Ambrogio, with his round pale cheeks and his lips closed tight. He jumped up, holding the photographs in his hands.

"There are some new elements, Signor Vicar," he said in a rush, "I believe this crime is connected to—"

"Perhaps I didn't explain myself clearly enough, Dottor De Luca," D'Ambrogio repeated and De Luca stopped in the middle of the room. "I thought that the chief made it perfectly clear this morning . . . The blurring of bureaus is not welcome. What are you doing here?"

"By chance, I found myself accompanying Maresciallo Pugliese . . . "

"I've already sent Maresciallo Pugliese to the station to write up a report of the events. I'll take care of him later. You, sir . . . What are you doing here?"

"By chance—"

"By chance, Dottor De Luca, you find yourself at the scene of a crime that has nothing to do with you and again, by chance, you find yourself in the middle of a nighttime shoot out. Bologna is not the Chicago of gangsters, Dottore. What are these new elements?"

De Luca stepped forward. He cleared his throat and tried not to spill everything out at once.

"Well, Signor Vicar, there may be a connection between Piras and the man killed in the brothel, insofar as—"

"First of all, the man at the brothel was not killed, he killed himself."

"Fine, but—"

"But nothing, De Luca! Nothing!" D'Ambrogio raised his

voice with a trill, and his cheeks filled with color. "That case is closed, it was a suicide and it doesn't concern us anymore! That communist they killed this morning is a homicide and it doesn't concern you, sir, but Dottor Bonaga and this here . . . " he swept his open hand around the room, "this mess here, for the time being is nothing more than an attempted robbery that once again does not concern you but the field operations bureau! Do you know what your job is, Special Sub Commissario De Luca? To chase whores, to ensure there are no minors working in the brothels, and to make certain they don't infect respectable people with the clap. Have I made myself clear, Dottore?"

D'Ambrogio was yelling. De Luca clenched his teeth to avoid yelling back. He would have liked to shout that there were too many things to sort out about this whole story, that he had discovered more clues in half a day that Bonaga could have found in a year, and that even if he was in vice he was still a cop, and a good cop. He would have liked to shout these things in D'Ambrogio's face, or even just to scream senselessly and nothing more, but instead he said nothing except "I'm not a dottore," quietly D'Ambrogio nodded, the blood ran from his cheeks. He took De Luca by the arm and pushed him toward the door.

"Go home," he said. "Get yourself some sleep and tomorrow, nice and easy, you can write your report about the shootout . . . Sober, no frills, the shootout and nothing else."

He held out a pale hand, which De Luca shook instinctively, and without expecting any kind of reply, repeating, "Go now, Special Sub Commissario, keep your mind on the whores, they're important too," he pushed De Luca out the door, almost tenderly.

Outside, the air was crisp; there had been a late spring cold snap, and De Luca pulled his trench coat closed around his neck, exhaling a plume of vapor. He walked around an empty jeep, which had been parked with two wheels on the sidewalk and put his foot on the running board. He noticed the same man he had first seen at Montagnola, the one in shirtsleeves bent over Piras's corpse. He stepped down off the sidewalk and stopped, turning his face to look over his shoulder.

"The man who fell off the roof . . . " he said quietly.

"Dead on impact. The suspected thief."

"The suspected thief, sure . . . Any marks on his face or hands?"

The man in shirtsleeves smiled.

"You mean scratches? He had two, here, on his cheek and one on the other side. Yes, your suspicions are right, Dottore."

De Luca smiled too. "I'm not a dottore," he mumbled and crossed the street. Behind him, D'Ambrogio came walking out of the building.

"Protest Over Weapons Seizure at Cavezzo di Modena."
"Seized Near Cesena Maderno, 81 mm Mortar with Ammunition, Two Hand Bombs, Two Machine Guns, Four Automatic Pistols."

"Fascist Squads Armed by Christian Democrats Attack Jews in the Roman Ghetto."

"Election Lottery: Everyone Can Play, Anyone Can Win a Prize. With 100 Lire You Could Win Millions. Lottery Tickets Running Out, Buy Now Before It's Too Late."

From his office window, De Luca could see the porticos of the building across the street. His window was on the first floor and through the wet stain on the glass that was expanding and shrinking with his every breath, De Luca could see through the eyes of the portico, right to the wall, veiled by that thin, intermittent fog. The wall under the portico was covered in posters, stuck almost on top of one another and brightly colored, a printer's rainbow that preceded the rain instead of following it, for the air that morning was shimmering gray, promising rainstorms. There was a red apelike energumen running across a map of Europe, his bare foot suspended over the outline of Italy, and above his head, the words "Careful! Communism Is Looking for a Boot!" There was another poster showing a hand tearing a crucifix from the insignia of the Christian Democrats and revealing underneath a bayonet. There, too, the word "Careful!" with a white border. Another poster, green and yellow, showed the faces of Rita Hayworth, Clark Gable and Tyrone Power, and above their faces, in red block letters, so small that De Luca had to squint to make them out, were the words "Even Hollywood Actors Are Among the Ranks of Those Fighting Communism!!!" and "Vote" written in large letters beneath it; a skull with empty eye sockets and a bearskin hat with a red star, "Vote, or He'll Be in Charge"; Garibaldi's face emerging from a star, "Peace, Liberty, Work. Vote for the Democratic Popular Front"; and another, with thick, white italics, like writing on a chalkboard, "In the Quiet of the Polling Booth, God Is Watching, Stalin Is Not!" and in yellow and black, "Defend Italy, In Russia Your Sons Belong to the State," and in red, "Stop This Crime from Happening. Vote National Bloc." "Peace, Work, Liberty, and Justice. Vote Democratic Popular Front." "A Vote for the Front Is a Vote on Two Fronts." "Peace, Work, and Liberty. Vote." "Church, Family, Work. Vote." "Italians . . . Vote, Make Others Vote, Vote Well."

De Luca walked away from the window. He sat down at his desk and leaned the back of his head against the wooden backrest and pushed, just to hear the pivot pin creak. He raised his eyes to the blades of the fan sitting on top of the file cabinet, covered by a furry film of gray dust, at the dead fly balanced on the edge of a map of Bologna hanging on the wall marked by red penciled circles indicating the various districts assigned to each station. He inhaled the odor of Lysol that the orderly had spread on the floor, the same odor he had encountered at Tripolina's brothel, but fainter. He thought about Ricciotti, and Piras, and Bonaga and the chief and shook his head, his teeth clenched. He leaned forward, making the chair's wood creak, put his elbows on the tabletop and his head in his hands, blowing air out through his fingers. He would have continued like that, blowing out all the air that he had in his lungs, in his heart, in his head, exhaling himself to death, perhaps, if Di Naccio hadn't knocked at the door.

De Luca looked at him as he came in and thought that some people are born with cops' faces. Maybe Brigadier Di Naccio had that same face in the crib, long and thin, and those sad oblique eyes, and that nose drooping down over his mouth. He wondered if his father had that same face, a station hound like him, pale skin, almost gray, his face stubbly, hurriedly and badly shaved early in the morning. Then he thought about himself, a lifetime on the force; raising an eyebrow he wondered if he too had that kind of face, a policeman's face. He touched his chin. It pricked his fingertips. He was reminded that he, on the other hand, hadn't shaved at all that morning.

"What is it?"

Di Naccio had a file in his hand, a thin folder, so thin it looked empty. It was green, like all the prostitutes' records, with Bologna Police Department written in pencil on the front and 18C written in the upper corner with a circle around it.

"Transfer papers," said Di Naccio. "Fifteen-day shift change."

"And so?"

"Every fifteen days the prostitutes have to change brothels and when they leave they must have a form that—"

"I know. I mean, why are you giving them to me? What do I have to do with them?"

"Rules say the ranking vice officer signs the papers, both incoming and outgoing . . . though your predecessor, Dottor Carapia, had me sign them all."

De Luca nodded, closing his eyes. Di Naccio had a deeply nasal timbre to his voice that annoyed De Luca. It was like his words came out of his nose, snorted out through his nostrils.

"Let's do the same, then," he said. "You sign them, that suits me fine."

"Of course, but . . . The same, I mean exactly the same as Dottor Carapia? *Exactly?*"

De Luca opened his eyes and looked at Di Naccio. He had one hand on the doorknob and that thin file between the thumb and forefinger of the other, as if it were scorching hot.

"Why?" he asked. "How did Dottor Carapia take care of it?"

"He wasn't really a stickler, Commissario . . . he closed the file even if something was missing. Here, for example, there's a transfer paper missing . . . "

All of a sudden, at the thought of the missing transfer paper, a sheet of flimsy carbon copy punched through by the type bars of an old typewriter with a worn out ribbon, identical to millions of other police papers and slips of paper that had passed through his hands, he clenched his teeth tight. He fought back the temptation to sweep everything from his desk, and for a moment he despaired at the idea of a life, or of just one day, spent hunting for missing 18Cs, for lost transfer papers, for forgotten stamps on #15 health certificates, at the thought of roundups, closing down brothels, of *the authority of the law enforcement bodies, in accordance with* and of all the useless and enervating discussions with maîtresses and prostitutes about all the possible interpretations of every comma in the Public Safety Act, Decree of 18 June 1931, Article 7; *On Prostitution.*

"Yes, fine," he said. "Let's just do the same, you take care of it."

He closed his eyes, putting his head back in his hands and his elbows on the desktop. He might have fallen asleep there and then if it were not for Di Naccio's voice droning in his ears, obliging him to listen even when the damned boy was talking to himself.

"Di Naccio . . . "

"Yes, sir, Commissario, sir."

"What did you say?"

"I said that I filed everything away in the record . . . "

"After that?"

" . . . in the record pertaining to the brothel in question. Tagliaferri Claudia. Via delle Oche, 16."

Fabbri Fiorina, known as La Wanda, born in Varese to Marcello and Maria, etc. etc. . . . destination, "Casa delle Rose," Palermo. Pistocchi Silvana, known as Mimì, destination "L'Orientale," Venice. Bianconcini Erminia, known as Gilda, destination, "57," via dei Fiori, Rome . . .

"When they change brothels, do they usually get scattered all over Italy like this?" asked De Luca. Di Naccio was standing behind him, hunched like a vulture over his shoulder so he could read the papers spread out on the desk. They were form papers, filled in with hesitant hands, and the more the handwriting was illegible, the further Di Naccio leaned over him. But neither of them took any notice.

"It happens," said Di Naccio. "The strange thing here is that they all moved so high up the ladder. L'Anitona is at the Superba in Genoa, la Triste at Fiori Chiari in Milan . . . 16 via delle Oche is a fifth rate dive, fifty lire for a simple, at Fiori Chiari you spend three hundred for the same treatment, but you should see the girls . . . " Di Naccio straightened up suddenly. "I know because I was stationed in Milan, Commissario, sir . . . "

"Yes, yes," De Luca mumbled, waving his hand in the air impatiently. "Show me which one's missing?"

"Look, here, it's this one. Here's the incoming paper, but no outgoing . . . "

Di Naccio leaned over De Luca's shoulder again. He put his finger on a piece of thick gray paper and moved it over the desk, sliding it across the other papers, creating a confused collage of "Bologna, on the . . . ," "Results of medical exam . . . ," "In good faith, the proprietor." The missing transfer belonged to Bianchi Lisa, known as Lisetta, born in Pieve di Cento, a suburb of Acquaviva, Ferrara province.

"Strange," said De Luca and thought back to the photograph, *Ermes and Lisetta, soon to be married.* He was about to start biting the inside of cheek again when he stopped and pressed his lips tight, perplexed. "Just a minute," he said. "Lisetta arrived a week ago. L'Anitona, la Wanda . . . " he looked over the other papers, rapid, "the entire group of fifteen arrived less than a week ago. Brigadier De Naccio, I admit that I'm new in vice, but a fifteen day shift ought to last fifteen days, even I know that much!"

Di Naccio lowered his gaze to the papers, leaning so far over De Luca that if anyone came in at that moment they would have thought him a two-headed cop, one head long and sad and the other curious and puzzled.

"Early turnover," said Di Naccio, straightening up again. He walked around the table, muttering, "there must be a reason, maybe, maybe . . . " and as De Luca watched him, he disappeared through the door. De Luca was about to call him back when he reentered the room with a piece of paper in his hand, a densely typed protocol, stamped and signed on one corner.

"It arrived this morning and I still have to file it," he said. "That's why I didn't remember straight off. 'The Bologna Police Department looks favorably on the transfer of the license in the name of Tagliaferri Claudia for via delle Oche 16 to the establishment at via dell'Orso 8.' Via dell'Orso is a ways up the ladder, second rate rather than fifth, that's why the owner transferred the girls early . . . "

"Just a second, Di Naccio, just a second . . . Who looked favorably on this change? Not us? Shouldn't it be this bureau looking favorably on matters of this nature?"

Di Naccio shrugged.

"Typically, yes, Commissario, sir . . . but this is signed by the chief's vicar." He raised his eyes to the ceiling, to the floors above, opening his arms wide.

De Luca bit his lip, lifting one eyebrow, then shook his head. He jumped out of the chair, making the pivot pin creak.

"Fine," he said. "If I have to take care of whores, then let me take care of them. Give me the transfer, I'm going to see what happened to this Lisetta."

"If the Front Wins, No Foreign Intervention Will Save Italy."

"Cardinal Lovitano, Monsignor Roberti, Monsignor Prisella Implicated in Yet Another Currency Scandal."

"First Run Opening Today at Nosadella: *The Bohemian Girl*, with Stan Laurel and Oliver Hardy."

A s he turned into via dell'Orso, pulling his trench coat around him to fend off a sudden gust of wind, De Luca thought that it really was an odd coincidence that the brothel on via delle Oche had been immediately dismantled and its girls scattered the length and breadth of Italy and, in a certain sense, promoted. And as he ran his eyes along the street numbers on the porcelain tiles, looking for number 8, he thought that the timely interest on the part of a vicar, a Christian Democrat to boot, in the affairs of a fifth-rate maîtresse, that reticent and almost arrogant Tripolina, she too promoted from via delle Oche to via dell'Orso, was even stranger.

He found the place open, the door partly closed. He pushed it open with the tip of his finger.

Sentimental . . . this endless night, this autumnal sky, this withered rose . . .

La Tripolina was on her knees on the floor, a rag in her hand, rubbing a stain on the large marble floor tiles. The foyer of via dell'Orso was nothing like the foyer of via delle Oche. Airy, well lit by a skylight, mirrors on the red walls, a round red velour sofa in the center of the room, and on either side of the staircase two columns of veined marble, also red. The only thing this place had in common with via delle Oche was la Tripolina. Still in her undergarments, her black hair tied in a bun at the back of her head, she was cleaning, just as he had seen her the morning before. This time, however, she was singing.

Sentimental . . . like a lost kiss, sentimental . . . like a sweet secret, sentimental . . . like a dream forever missed . . .

La Tripolina was happy. It was clear from the tone in her voice, from the feeling she put in her song, whispered, her mouth barely open. She made De Luca smile. He crossed his arms over the file and rather than coughing into his closed fist, twice, as he had intended, he waited a while, watching her.

Like this goodbye, that breaks the heart . . . sentimental . . . sentimental . . .

La Tripolina straightened up, sitting back on her bare heels, and turned to look over her shoulder.

"Peep show costs seventy-five lire," she said, harsh, "but you'll have to come back, we're closed."

De Luca blushed. "Excuse me," he mumbled, his face on fire. Then he shook his head, coughed twice into his fist as he had planned to do, and entered the foyer with resolve, striding in like a commissario from the vice bureau. La Tripolina, meanwhile, had stood up and slipped into her flannel slippers that were sitting on the floor. She picked up her black shawl from the back of a chair, and the sweeping movement with which she threw it over her shoulder sent a flurry of air onto De Luca's face and lifted the lock of hair that had fallen over her forehead, almost to her eyes.

"Nice," said De Luca, looking around. "A nice change, really." He nodded, resting his gaze on a coat rack with hooks in the form of phalluses. "Classy, too."

"What do you want from me?"

"Lisetta's outgoing transfer papers."

"I don't have them."

"Why not?"

"She left without a word."

"Why?"

"Maybe she went back home. Maybe she found a husband."

"And she disappears just like that? She was here the other day then *poof!* Out of the blue, with no medical certificate . . . "

"Maybe she didn't want to take the medical."

"This could get you in trouble, Tripolina."

"Not . . . " la Tripolina stopped short, closing her full lips around a sigh, her mouth shaped as if for a kiss. She shrugged, lowering her gaze, her eyes disappeared for a moment under her creased brow. "Do whatever you want."

De Luca touched her under the chin with the edge of the dossier. He brushed against her lightly, but her head shot up as if he had given her a slap.

"Were you about to say, 'not with the protection I've got'?" De Luca said. "I know you've got a saint watching over you, if not, you wouldn't be here. I know: if I start getting on your case with medical and hygiene visits, orders to come to the station, stamps and countersignatures on permits, sooner or later, someone's going to come out of the woodwork, maybe even a vicar, and he'll tell me to use my office resources more efficiently. So, you know what I'm going to do? Do you know, Tripolina?"

De Luca walked by her and turning on his heels he sat down on the sofa in the middle of the room, making the red cushions sigh.

"I'm going to come here every night. I'm single, I'm free, with all that's happened to me I haven't even touched a woman for over a year . . . Surely I have a right to spend my free nights as I please, no? So I'm going to come here, just like this, with my hat on my knees . . . " he put his knees together, sat up straight and stiff, his arms in his lap, "I really don't wear a hat, but I'll put one on just the same, because it makes me look more like a policeman . . . Then I'm going to look everyone who comes in here in the eyes, like this . . . " he planted his eyes on Tripolina, frowning and pulling his lips into a suspicious and arrogant smile, a cop's smile. "And then, you know what I'm going to do? Later in the night, I'm going to get Di Naccio to join me . . . Do you know brigadier Di Naccio, you ever seen that face of his? And to make things even clearer, I'll get him to say, 'fine, sir, Commissario, sir.' That's all . . . who knows, maybe every so often I'll get my notepad out and jot something down . . . "

La Tripolina's eyes were shining, black behind a veil of tears. She pressed her lips together tight, as if in that way she could hold back her tears, so tight that from the dark, almost olive color they usually were, her lips turned white. She'd grabbed the corners of her shawl, holding them in her fists and the black wool, pulled tight over her shoulder, had pushed her slip off one shoulder, leaving it bare. De Luca swallowed, lowering his gaze from the sight of her smooth, dark flesh.

"Come on Tripolina, let's stop this," he said. "I want to know what Ricciotti was up to in the days before he died."

"I don't know. I haven't seen him since Saturday. Sunday was his day off and he didn't come back after that."

"Fine. I want to know how you got your license transferred from via delle Oche to here."

"I gave D'Ambrogio a tip off. People talk when they're in bed and at the moment idle chatter is worth something."

"What kind of idle chatter?"

"I don't know. Communists. Things that Lisetta knew about."

"Fine. Now I want to know why Piras photographed Ricciotti with Lisetta and all those other girls."

La Tripolina sighed, with an incomplete sob, like a child's, and smiled.

"Ermes played the hired fiancé, for the families. Sometimes we get girls who work in the business without telling anyone at home, like Lisetta, and they need a fiancé to reassure their parents. Ermes had a suit and he came off as a decent boy . . . that's it. Is there anything else you want to know?"

De Luca shook his head. "No," he said. "Nothing for the time being. But you'll see, I'll be back."

"I know," she murmured. She kneeled down beside him, a movement De Luca wasn't expecting, and reached for his hand. She held it in hers, without malice, tight and without looking at him, without saying a word. She leaned her head on his knees and closed her eyes with a sigh, as if she would have liked to fall asleep right there. De Luca didn't move. He sat there stiffly, at a loss for what to do. Through the fabric of his trousers he felt the warmth of Tripolina's cheek on his leg. In that position, with her eyelids closed and her lips barely open, so near and so strange, she seemed less battered and worn than before. She could have been thirty, la Tripolina, and in that moment he thought she was decidedly pretty.

She heard it first and she raised her head quickly, opening her eyes, her nostrils flaring as if she were sniffing the air. One step, preceded by the sound of the door opening, one clack of a heeled shoe on the marble floor tiles that made De Luca turn on the sofa. La Tripolina stood up fast, smoothing out her slip over her knees.

From closer up, cabinet chief Scala seemed shorter than when De Luca had met him in the briefing room the day before. He was wearing the same gray double-breasted suit, no tie, a white shirt open at the neck, and in his eyes the same bemused look.

"Commissario De Luca?" he said. "Brigadier Di Naccio told me I might find you here. Shall we take a little walk?"

"AGITPROP IN CHURCH. OR RATHER, THE TACTICS OF GOSSIP MON-GERING. WIDESPREAD EFFORTS OF COMMUNISM TO INFILTRATE THE FEMININE MASSES."

"OFFICE WORKERS VOTE FOR THE FRONT. A FRONT VICTORY WILL GIVE US DEMOCRATIC SCHOOLS."

"GUESTS STOPPING BY? BIANCOSARTI LIQUOR IS DE RIGUEUR."

A raindrop hit De Luca in the middle of his head, sliding down his scalp, cold and irritating. Scala held out his arm, his palm up, and lifted his face to the sky, his eyes closed.

"Rain," he said. "Let's hope it's bad weather on Sunday too."

"Sunday?" De Luca asked.

"The elections. If it rains the bigots stay at home, and De Gaspari is screwed . . . On the other hand, we, all of us, will be going to vote. By 'we' I mean we communists, Dottore."

"I'm not a dottore."

Scala pointed to the arches at the end of via dell'Orso and the two men stopped beneath them, watching the raindrops that were beginning to smack against the cobblestones.

"I'm a country boy," said Scala. "And where I'm from, the rain smells different, like iron . . . wet iron. Here in Bologna, it smells like dust. How are the investigations going? Have you figured out who killed Ricciotti and Piras?"

"Yes, Piras was killed by a man who then fell from a roof, a man who had scratch marks on his face from Piras's finger-nails. And he killed Piras because he wanted certain photo-graphs."

"Photographs, you say. Why's that, precisely?"

"Because we don't know exactly what he was looking for but we know where he was looking. He opened Piras's camera and the only things he could have been looking for there are photographs."

"And what is in these photographs?"

"We don't know."

"And where were they taken?"

"We don't know."

"And Ricciotti?"

"Ricciotti knew Piras. He knew him well."

"Thus, one could presume that the crimes are connected and that both men were killed by the same person?"

"One could presume that, yes."

"You are being rather vague, Commissario De Luca."

"I don't know how I could be otherwise, Dottor Scala. I have no resources at my disposal, no information, I continual-ly come up against a wall of silence and the minute I try to take a step forward, they stop me. And, then, I'm not with the homicide bureau, I'm in vice, and the vicar told me—"

"The vicar, the vicar . . . What a strange name for a police-man. The chief of police's vicar! The bishop's vicar . . . It smacks of the church, don't you find?"

De Luca shrugged, his gaze lost in the rain shower that was growing heavier and more violent by the minute. Scala moved further beneath the arches stretching across the street, like a portico cut in two, and pulled his jacket closed around him, shivering.

"You know who the man on Piras's roof was?" he said. "I bet the vicar didn't tell you that."

"No," said De Luca, then he repeated himself, because anxiety was tightening his throat and he wasn't able to raise his voice over the sound of the rain. "No, he didn't tell me."

"Matteucci . . . Silvano, I believe. But his name isn't important. He was one of the Little Abbot's men. You know who the Little Abbot is, right?"

De Luca shook his head, silent.

"The late Home and Church's pet. He's the secretary of a civic committee that operated as a campaign office for Orlandelli. If you want to know more, ask Marconi, in the political squad. Get Brigadier Sabatini from forensics to show you the films and tell him that I sent you. You want an autopsy? Mr. Cinelli, at the coroners . . . Here in Bologna we're still strong in the police department. Our boys are all at your disposal, Commissario De Luca, take advantage of them . . . take advantage of the K factor."

The sound of the rain had become a roar. The rain was falling so thick and heavy that the air in front of them looked like a wall slanting sideways, and beyond the street the porticos of via Galliera had disappeared. De Luca pressed his lips together and passed his hand over his face. The drops that bounced off the arches and made their way underneath shone on his unshaved chin.

"If I were in homicide," yelled Scala, "I'd ask why this Matteucci was emptying out a comrade's house instead of being out on the street sticking up anti-communist posters. You, sir, wouldn't you ask yourself the same thing? I'll tell you what, I'll get Bonaga sent to Rome for a little while and in the meantime you ask yourself that question, De Luca, you go ahead and ask it . . . "

Scala squeezed his arm, then flicked up the collar of his double-breasted suit, pulled his head down between his shoulders and disappeared beneath the rain toward the porticos of via Galliera. De Luca started, opened his trench coat and slipped in the green file, by now so wet it seemed black. He leaned against the wall, threw his arms around himself, and stood there, wrapped up in his trench coat; him, the cold shivers, the insomnia, and all those transferred whores, minus one. Biting his cheek, he wrinkled his brow and started to think.

APRIL 16 1948
FRIDAY

"WARNING FOR THE UNDECIDED: VOTE AND VOTE ITALIAN." "16 MIL-LION SLAVES IN THE SOVIET LABOR CAMPS." "WEAPONS FOUND IN THE RENO CANAL."

"200 THOUSAND PEOPLE IN NAPLES FOR COMRADE TOGLIATTI'S SPEECH." "IF THE CHRISTIAN DEMOCRATS WIN ALL OF ITALY WILL BE A SEMINARY: NO MORE CHARLIE CHAPLIN, TOTÒ, OR RITA HAY-WORTH. YOU'LL DIE OF BOREDOM."

"TODAY AT THE MANZONI: ROBERT TAYLOR, LANA TURNER IN *JOHN-NY EAGER*. GLUE YOUR MOVIE TICKET TO YOUR ELECTION LOTTERY TICKET TO WIN ONE OF 200 THOUSAND CONSOLATION PRIZES."

T hey call him Abatino, the Little Abbot, because that's his surname . . . Abatino, Antonio Abatino. And also because he really does look like a little abbot . . . there he is, there."

The film had no sound track, except for the noise of the projector, a jerky drone, intense and contained, that went unnoticed after a few minutes. There was too much light in the room, though the windows had been closed, and the black and white footage faded into a uniform pale gray that made their eyes ache. "Don't expect the big screen, Dottore," Brigadier Sabatini had told him as he closed the shutters, "this is the office of the forensics unit, not a movie cinema." He was behind the projector now, together with Marconi from the political squad, who kept saying, "There he is there, you see him? Behind Orlandelli, the Right Honorable Home and Church . . . Did you see him, Dottore?"

De Luca was sitting on a wooden stool, his arms resting on his knees, leaning forward toward the white sheet stretched on the wall by four nails at the corners. Next to him, perched on a munitions crate with "US Army" printed in white on the green metal, was Pugliese. The light from the projector cut them in half, sending the curved shadows of their profiles onto the two sides of the scene, like an ornamental frieze, spectral and asymmetrical, framing the film. Long silent tracking shots that were interrupted by fits and starts as the cameraman focused showed a rally in Piazza Maggiore. It was raining and the iron-colored sky blended with the doughy white trench coats, the gray faces, and the faded black jackets.

"Jesus, this footage is really the pits," said Pugliese.

There was a man in the foreground standing under an umbrella, an old man. He was standing on a wooden stage, covered to his waist by loudspeakers as he spoke into a flat, square microphone suspended in the middle of a metal ring. He had gray hair and a small, thin face, but from his open mouth beneath the white shadow of a moustache, from his clenched fists held in front of his face, from the movement of his head, fast, his eyes closed, it was obvious that he was shouting, forcefully. A mute cry, erased by the steady drone of the projector that also replaced the crowd's applause, shown in a slow pan from the sea of umbrellas in one part of the piazza to the police battalions in helmets with automatic rifles over their shoulders, stationed at the foot of the steps to San Petronio.

"All that screaming about communists eating babies," said Marconi, "in the end Orlandelli had a stroke. They say that when they found him dead at his desk—"

"No comments, Brigadier," said De Luca, stern. "I don't see this Abatino . . . Can we go back?"

"He'll be back, now, Dottore," said Sabatini, "the camera turns back to the stage . . . There, the one with the umbrella."

Now that he saw him, De Luca didn't think Abatino looked anything like a little abbot. He was wearing a light-colored suit, similar to the one he himself was wearing, a white shirt collar and a black tie. He was young, Antonio Abatino, thin; he had a large nose, a mass of hair combed straight back. He wore glasses, a pair of lightweight glasses with round lenses that turned opaque when he turned toward the camera. He held his umbrella with his arm stiff, as if it were a sword, holding it over Orlandelli, who was still yelling. Then the camera moved down, to the foot of the stage, and focused on a placard soaked with rain bearing a coat of arms with two hands joined in front of the outline of a church. The camera remained focused on the wording: "Giving your vote to parties that profess doctrine contrary to the Catholic faith means committing a mortal sin."

"Pay attention, Dottore . . . Here comes the other one."

The camera zoomed out to capture a group of people who had entered the piazza. They were all men and they too had umbrellas in their hands, but the umbrellas were closed. Some of them wore red bandanas around their necks. One of them, tall and large, in shirtsleeves and a visored cap, had pushed his way to the side of the stage and was waving his fist and yelling, mute. The Little Abbot moved around to the other side of the Right Honorable Orlandelli, to serve as a shield.

"Did you see him, Pugliese?" asked De Luca.

"Yeah, I saw him," Pugliese said.

"I don't mean Abatino."

"Neither do I, Commissa."

In the corner of the screen, more faded than the rest of the footage but visible nonetheless, a man had entered the shot. He face had leapt into the clearer grays, where the camera was better focused, displaying his profile, his curly hair falling over his forehead, his nose crooked, his jaw square. It was the

man who had fallen from the roof. The camerawork had started to get jumpy and the scene was a blur, but right before
stepping out of the scene, the camera panning away from him,
the man had approached Abatino with a closed umbrella in
his hands.

"Matteucci Silvano," said Marconi, "former junior officer
of the Decima Mas. Prior convictions for public disturbance,
assault, and attempted murder. After the war he was in the
black market. Officially, now he's a vagrant."

"The chief gets us to film everything," said Sabatini. "From
the Pilgrim Madonna processions to the rallies held by the
Popular Front. Equal treatment, he says, that way he's solid
with everyone."

De Luca lifted his hand up into the beam of light coming
from the projector.

"Leave us alone for a moment, please," he said. He leaned
in toward Pugliese, placing the shadow of his upper body
across the men yelling silently on the screen. "And you, Maresciallo? Are you solid?"

The camera panned across the stage, crooked and fast, a
tide of umbrellas and closed fists, of hats, berets, caps, and helmets, glistening under the rain.

"I have a family, Commissa," said Pugliese.

"So do I. This is my family." De Luca opened his arms wide,
lifting them up to indicate the walls. "And it's yours, too,
Maresciallo Pugliese. We're policemen."

"No. I'm a policeman with a wife and a baby boy to bring
up on a maresciallo's salary, and I can't afford to be transferred
to Sicily to hunt down the bandit Giuliano . . ."

"We're covered, Pugliese. That's not going to happen. Scala
is going to keep D'Ambrogio and Bonaga off our backs for a
while."

Pugliese smiled. A sardonic smile that replaced the worried
expression he had on his face.

"So, you're working with the communists, Commissa? You know, they're going to lose the elections . . ."

On the screen, the police jeeps cut silently through the crowd, which opened before them and dispersed in all directions, running, toward the porticos, toward the stairs to San Petronio, toward the fountain of Neptune. On the jeeps, standing on the seats and holding fast to the windshield, uniformed policemen were striking the air with their batons, slow, like a ballet without music.

"I'm not working with anyone!" De Luca growled. "I'm doing my job, which is to investigate a case, and I'm going to keep doing it until I discover who the murderer is!"

"Why, do you think Scala gives a damn about who killed Ricciotti and Piras? This matter interests Scala because it interests Abatino! Commissa, we're heading into elections, this is all about politics! They're using you, too."

"I don't give a damn if they use me! I'm a policeman, Pugliese, it's my job and I'll take sides with anyone who lets me do my job."

He realized he was screaming more by the offended look on Pugliese's face than by the sound of his voice bouncing off the walls. Behind him, on the screen, the image had gone cloudy with smoke from the teargas that had been fired into the piazza, now swarming with people running between clouds of white smoke.

"Is that why," hissed Pugliese, coolly, "you sided with the fascists? Is that how you ended up in the investigative unit of the Muti? When I met you, Commissa, your name was on a list of people that the partisans were going to put in front of a firing squad. Remember?"

The film had jammed, with a long, thin whine of the straining motor. For a few seconds, a man out of focus in shirtsleeves running toward the camera remained on the screen, behind his back the thick clouds of smoke, a policeman on the hood of a jeep, his baton lifted. Just a couple of seconds, then the image curled into a black hole that spread out from the center, smoking.

"Fuck you, Maresciallo Pugliese! Now I'm a member of the police force of the Italian Republic and I'm investigating a murder. Are you with me or not?"

"Fuck you, too, Commissario De Luca, sir! You know I am!"

They were staring at each other, both surly and flushed, Pugliese stern and De Luca panting. They looked at each for a long time, without noticing the repeated slapping of the film that had come off the spool or the pungent smell of burnt celluloid. De Luca looked away. He stood up from the stool and put his hand on Pugliese's shoulder.

"Wire all the police departments involved," he said, "and the carabinieri. Get them a list of questions to ask the prostitutes that used to work in via delle Oche. I want profiles on Ricciotti and the rest of them, including this Little Abbot. I want to go back to via delle Oche, to speak to Armida and all the others. And I want Lisetta, wherever she is. Let's go, Pugliese. Time to get to work."

"GIANT CINZANINO YELLOW CAP CONTEST." "SANLEY LIGHT WINE ON THE ROCKS: FINE, THIRST-QUENCHING LIQUOR." "ORANGE + SUGAR = MARTINAZZI SODA: MAY COST MORE, SURELY THE BEST." "WANT TO LIVE AS LONG AS NOAH? DON'T DRINK COFFEE, DRINK VECCHINA."

A t least drink something . . . A Cinzanino? A dab of vermouth? A drop of Cognac? *Fanny!*"
The kitchen of number 23 smelled of meat sauce. L'Armida had called it the administrative office but the only thing in the room that looked remotely administrative was a wide-ruled bookkeeping form covered with numbers, and a pile of medical certificates stacked on a corner of the table. As for the rest, it was a kitchen, and the carrots and onions frying in a saucepan on the hotplate of a white enamel stove filled the air with the heavy, greasy smell of oil. De Luca sat down beside the table, in front of the hotplate, but then stood right back up because his still empty stomach cramped up with an angry growl. He leaned against the sink, folding his trench coat over his arms, which he held tightly over his stomach to stop it from rumbling. His throat tensed and a hot, growling sensation of hunger alternated with another, equally hot and overwhelming, of nausea.

"But Commissario, why are you standing? The chair's no good? I'll have another one brought in . . . *Fanny!*"

L'Armida clapped her hands and De Luca shook his head, no, no, and waved his hands when she insisted.

"No, just have that other woman brought in," he said. "The one who found the body." L'Armida nodded gravely, making her double chin dance.

"As you wish . . . Fanny! Get Caty to bring the commissario his cinzanino!"

"Let's get back to the matter at hand," Pugliese said, quickly, because De Luca had turned his face to the ceiling, smothering a curse that was on his lips. "You were telling us about Ermes . . ."

"Such a good boy, Signor Maresciallo. A little coarse, maybe, but a good boy. I tell you, a good boy . . . Maybe a little unlucky. Had trouble with the police, but he came to his senses a while back. He said he wanted to find a real job, get married, start a family . . . But I can't tell you much about that night, Signor Commissario. You yourself saw where poor Ermes's room is, up there, in that little tower kind of thing, separate from the house . . . Who could have heard him from here! Wait . . . maybe Ivonne. She's in the room up against the wall of the tower . . . I'll call her in now. *Ivonne!*"

De Luca screwed up his face and closed his eyes. A hot wave washed through his stomach, helped along by a growl of hunger that was extinguished fast when the odor of meat sauce blended with the tangy, bubbling smell of the cinzano.

"Ivonne?" he asked, at a loss, but the girl standing next to him with a tray in her hands shook her head, making her bobbed hair rustle against the chiffon collar of her dressing gown.

"No, I'm Caty." She turned to Pugliese. "Monteschi Carmelina, Maresciallo . . ."

"Caty, give the commissario his cinzanino like a good girl and tell him about Ermes . . ."

"Oh God, what an awful thing! I'm still all upset about it, poor boy. Who would have imagined . . . Don't you want your cinzanino? Would you let me look under the cap?"

"Caty, go add a little water to the commissario's drink . . . Or would you like something nonalcoholic? *Fanny!*"

"Here I am, Signora. You called?"

"No, thank you. Listen, Fanny . . ." De Luca began, but the girl who had just come into the room shook her head too, as she closed her velour dressing gown over her breast

"I'm not Fanny. I'm Ivonne." And to Pugliese, she said: "Anconelli Ivonne, known as Gigì . . . put the stress on the final i, wont you? Otherwise it's Gigi and it sounds like I'm a transvestite. It's Gigì, with the g like in French, gzi-gzì . . . You know, my mother was from Paris."

"Ivonne, be a good girl and tell the commissario about Ermes . . . Dottore, would you prefer a coffee? I'll have one made for you . . . *Fanny!*"

"That's enough!" cried De Luca, throwing his arms open. "I don't want anything, thank you! I just want to know how this Ermes was acting lately. Was he worried, scared, elated, mad at someone? . . . I want to know if it looked like his spirits were up or down."

Caty and Ivonne spoke at the same time, almost with the same pitch to their voices.

"Up," said Caty.

"Down," said Ivonne.

"His spirits were up, like she said . . . He was euphoric."

"No, Caty, he was down . . . His mood was as black as a hat, I tell you."

"Listen, Commissario, it's not that I was ever very close to the boy, but he'd been real talkative lately, he was always turning around on his Vespa, monkeying around, and he scared me . . . Watch the road, I told him. And he'd just say, Who cares! And he was always singing . . ."

"Believe me, Commissario, I heard Ermes the other night, clear as a bell . . . Back and forth in his room like a caged animal and at a certain point he let fly with a flurry of punches against the wall. I even called out to him but he just told me to go sell my ass. Then I heard him crying. Then nada, 'cause when I finish my shift I take a Luminal and sleep like a log."

"Ah, so, you were sleeping before as well . . . Listen to me, Commissario. A few days ago, while he was taking me to novena, Ermes said: Caty, I'm going to be leaving soon. I'm getting married and I'm going to open a gym in San Lorenzo. Then he sang 'Red Flag'[1] all the way from here to San Petronio . . . What an embarrassment, Commissario. That was the day after the storm . . ."

"You dreamed the storm . . ."

"No. You're the one with the room up front and with the windows closed you wouldn't know if it was raining or snowing . . . Plus, Signor Commissario, even if she did open them . . . She calls it Luminal, but where I come from we call it morphine."

"No, it's all that cognac buzzing in your ears that makes you see lightning . . ."

"Hey, hey, girls!"

L'Armida clapped her hands and once more De Luca closed his eyes. He couldn't take that tight little kitchen anymore, and that racket, greasy with meat sauce and fizzy with cinzano. Outside on the street, he freed his lungs with a deep breath that made his head light and empty and cleared his vision. Then he threw his hands into the pockets of his trench coat and waited for Pugliese.

"Now that's what they call a cathouse, Commissa. What are you thinking?"

"About a guy who's over the moon one day about something that's going to change his life and the next day, no. Where was he that day? And where was he the next day? Where was he on Sunday?"

---

[1] *Bandiera Rossa* (Red Flag) is a traditional left-wing Italian folk song.

"Shit, who knows? We don't even know if there was a storm on Sunday or not."

"Who gives a good god damn about the storm, Pugliese."

"TODAY, CLOSING RALLIES AT MIDNIGHT. ALL LIPS SEALED. SUNDAY AND MONDAY, TRAM SERVICES RUN AN HOUR AHEAD. THREE DAYS' PAID HOLIDAY FOR ALL WORKERS. HOLY MASSES AN HOUR EARLIER ON ELECTION DAY."

Wire #126, attn. Bologna Station, Vice. From: Pieve di Cento (FE) Carabinieri post. Inform officer responsible that Bianchi Lisa, known as Lisetta, is currently not to be found at her family home. Further inquiry impossible at present due to deployment of personnel in ground control for upcoming parliamentary elections . . .

"De Luca? Hello? It's Razzini, from the Rome station . . . Listen, colleague, I've got the things you asked me for on Gilda. I'll read it to you. Okay . . . she answers: *No, I didn't notice anything strange concerning the above-mentioned Ricciotti Ermes, whose suicide I only learned about upon my arrival in Rome. I hasten to add that I noticed nothing unusual during my stay in Bologna. Faithfully . . .* What do you mean, 'is that all?' My boy, we're heading into elections. I had a hard time even getting a lance-corporal out there . . ."

"Commissario De Luca? Brigadier Mordiglia, Genoa vice. Let me just point out that we are short on personnel as we're heading into the elections and in two hours Togliatti is speaking in the square . . . I'll get to the point. I personally interrogated Anitona and I can convey the following declaration to you. *I didn't notice anything strange concerning the above mentioned Ricciotti Ermes, whose suicide I only learned about upon my arrival in Genoa. I hasten to add that I noticed nothing unusual during my stay in Bologna.* Everything in order, Commissario? I'm in a hurry. All best to you, too . . ."

Right, Fabbri Fiorina, known as Wanda, Signor Commissario . . . answers: *I didn't notice anything strange concerning the above mentioned Ricciotti Ermes, whose suicide I only learned about upon my arrival in—* Yes, indeed, only upon her arrival in Palermo. How did you know? Don't tell me they've already sent this through? With all we have to do today . . ."

Wire #138, att'n Bologna Station, Vice. From: San Lazzaro Carabinieri post. Concerning your request re: Bianchi Lisa, known as Lisetta. We inform you that the above mentioned Bianchi Lisa is currently to be found in a locality within our jurisdiction . . ."

Lisetta really did seem like a child, and maybe she still was; tiny, blond, her hair tied in two thin pigtails and ribs sticking out of her bony body, like a little girl's, still undernourished from the war days. Perhaps her eyes were even blue, the blue eyes of a babe, but in that position, her eyes wide open and rolled back in her head as they were, De Luca could only see their whites. She was naked, except for a pair of stockings.

"She suffocated to death, Commissa," said Pugliese. Leaning over the bed that was jammed up against a wall, his face was right next to Lisetta's, almost as if he wanted to kiss her. "And if no one else had a hand in her death, for once?"

De Luca looked around the room. It was small, four barren walls stained with mold that contained a folding bed, an overturned trunk, and a porcelain enameled basin. Beneath the metal stand supporting the basin there was a pair of sandals with a cork heel, tiny, with a red border. On the bed, her legs hanging over the iron frame, her arms open, naked on the mattress, was Lisetta. The tips of her toes, covered in stockings, were lightly touching a pillow with a red stain.

"I don't think so," he said. "There's lipstick on the pillow case and I doubt that she had been kissing the pillow. Look over there."

De Luca pointed to the floor. Against the wall, in a corner, there was a broken tile sticking up. Only one.

"They didn't even need to beat her up. She must have told them straight off, poor Lisetta. Lot of good it did her."

"What did she have hidden there, Commissa? The photographs? And what the fuck was in those photographs?"

Lisetta's room was at the top of a crumbling house that had been half destroyed by bombing during the war. Wooden stairs nailed to a balcony led up to the room. They had creaked under first Pugliese's and then De Luca's footsteps, and were creaking again now under the footsteps of a carabiniere.

"Are you done, Dottore?" he said, sticking his head into the room. "I mean, if it were up to us you could stay as long as you wanted, but any moment now the procession of the Pilgrim Madonna will be passing through here and as the communists want to block the street and the car you have is so obviously a police car . . ."

"Commissa, what the fuck were in those photos?" Pugliese repeated, turning to face De Luca. "De Gaspari at dinner with Stalin?"

They left the driving to Sabatini, just in case, and De Luca sat in the back, sunk into the studded backrest of the black Fiat 1100. He'd quit biting the inside of his cheek because although the road from San Lazzaro to Bologna was paved it was pockmarked with large unpaved blotches that more than once brought the sickly-sweet taste of blood to the back of his teeth.

"We need to find out where they were taken. Where was Piras the day that Ricciotti bought the farm?"

"The day of the storm."

"You're obsessed with that storm. Forget about the damn storm. Where were Ricciotti and Piras? At a campaign rally? At a street fight? At dinner with De Gasperi and Stalin, as you suggest? What do we know about these people? Let's get back to the station and have a look at Marconi's files . . . What's happening down there?"

Sabatini had hit the brakes. The car was moving forward slowly. Up ahead there was a group of people standing beside a cart. A man armed with a pitchfork was dumping bales of hay onto the road. One of the other men left the group, straddled a motorbike and came toward the car.

"Let me do the talking," said Sabatini, winding down the window. The man on the motorbike stopped in front of the car and leaned down over the handlebars to look inside. He may have recognized Sabatini because even before saying anything he nodded once.

"Let them through," he yelled. "They're comrades." He saluted, throwing his closed fist in the air. Sabatini stuck his arm out through the open window and Pugliese lifted his left hand, too, bringing his fist up close to his face. De Luca, bouncing up and down as the car drove over the hay, bit into his bloody cheek again. It looked to him as if one of the men behind the cart had something sticking up from behind his shoulder, like the black barrel of a rifle. But he turned away and pretended not to notice.

"MACHINE GUN FIRES ON AIRPLANE BELONGING TO NATIONAL BLOC." "CONCERNING THE PROHIBITION ON HOLDING RALLIES IN FACTORIES."

"THE MARSHALL PLAN WILL IMPEDE SOCIAL REFORM."

"TOMORROW AT THE ELISEO: SPENCER TRACY AND MICKEY ROONEY IN *MEN OF BOYS TOWN*."

Here are the files, Commissa . . . Marconi didn't want to give them to me, then he called Scala and things worked out. Right . . . Ricciotti Ermes, born in San Lazzaro in Bologna Province in 1928. Son of communist workers, both killed in the bombing. Between 1946 and 1947 he was arrested and charged several times for larceny, assault with intent, receiving stolen goods, and contempt. Since '48 both vice and the political squad have him listed as an employee of the bordello in via delle Oche, 16, etc. etc. The boys from the political squad tell us that he's a communist sympathizer and sure enough there's a bunch of paperwork in here about his career as an amateur boxer, about his request for recognition as a partisan being refused, but nothing about his frequenting Piras's photographic studio in via Marconi 33. Strange, don't you think, Commissa . . ."

"And now to Piras, Commissa . . . Osvaldo Piras, son of Gavino, deceased, born in Sassari in 1902. In '25 he emigrates to the continent, stopping first in Rome and then in Bologna, where he works in his uncle's photography studio. Uncle's a fascist opponent and in '26 he ends up in the slammer. Nephew Osvaldo takes over the studio. In '29 he too is arrested by the Militia but released immediately. There's a note written in pencil and signed by Bologna Chief of Police D'Andrea saying that anything concerning Piras Osvaldo, son of Gavino, deceased, is to be passed directly to the OVRA. Then, nothing until 1947 when Piras joins the Italian Communist Party and here we have another penciled note, no signature this time, saying that all enquiries concerning Piras should be directed to the political squad. And you know who the director of the Political Squad was in '47? D'Ambrogio. Strange, don't you think, Commissa?"

"Here it is, Commissa. That Matteucci Silvano was a first-rate bastard. After the war they wanted to put him in front of a firing squad but he saved his skin by giving himself up to the Allies. In '45 he was sentenced to twelve years, reduced to six following an appeal, then he got himself released as part of the amnesty. Officially, he's a street pedlar, but according to political he served as a strong arm for whoever wanted him, from the MSI[1] to the Uomo Qualunque. It doesn't say here that he worked for Abatino, but, you want to know what's written in Abatino's file? Nothing. Just one line, beneath the vital statistics. One line that reads: 'Sympathizer with parties for public order.' Isn't that strange, Commissa?"

[1] *Movimento Sociale Italiano*. Founded in 1946 by former exponents of the Italian Social Republic (otherwise known as the "Salò Republic" or simply "Salò"), the MSI was a neo-fascist political party. (Tr.)

"How To Crush Freedom: Eight National Bloc Bill-Posters Brutally Beaten by Communists in Imola."

"Catholic Action Youth Tries to Kill a Comrade. Assailant Confesses: 'I Wanted to Do Him In Because He's a Communist.'"

The boy turned the throttle and the Lambretta let out a hoarse croak, like a cough. It seemed to stall, and the boy stood up on the footboard, leaning over the handlebars like a cyclist on a climb, and persisted, turning the throttle until the roar became steady, an angry growl punctuated every now and again by a sputter.

Antonio Abatino nodded, shielding his mouth from the exhaust fumes invading the garage.

"All right," he said. "But will it manage to pull all of this?"

There was a handcart attached to the Lambretta. In the middle of the handcart there was a wooden bust. Garibaldi's face had been pulled off the bust and attached, like a mask, to a hinged arm. Every movement of the handcart sent the arm bobbing up and down, revealing what was behind Garibaldi's face; Stalin's face, topped by his red-starred cap. "Watch Out for Fraud" said a sign on the side of the handcart, intentionally written in childish handwriting that reminded De Luca, still standing at the door with Pugliese, of his school notebooks.

"Antonio Abatino?" De Luca said. The noise from the Lambretta covered his voice. "Antonio Abatino," he repeated. "Sub Commissario De Luca and Maresciallo Pugliese, police."

A few seconds passed before Abatino turned, slowly, as if he'd been trying to decide whether to do so or not. He looked at De Luca, then Pugliese, moving his head slightly on a stiff neck. The sunlight reflecting off the garage door turned the lenses of his glasses opaque, just like in the projection.

"Shall we turn that scooter off?" Pugliese asked. Abatino shook his head, his neck still stiff.

"Rather not," he said. "The motor has to warm up. What can I do for you?"

"What is this place?" asked De Luca, lifting a finger and rotating it in the air. The fumes from the Lambretta were growing strong, irritating, the acid stink of gas oil. Abatino didn't make a move but for an almost imperceptible tightening around the corners of his mouth. His thin face was marked by two deep creases running down either side of his nose and mouth and one of them, for a brief instant, wrinkled slightly.

"This place is the headquarters of the Civic Committee, of which I am the Secretary. Via del Porto, number 18."

"Isn't there somewhere more comfortable where we can speak?" De Luca asked, and he was about to take a step forward but Abatino didn't move from where he was standing, just inside the door. His arms hung down, motionless on either side of his black coat, which was buttoned all the way up. His long straight legs were clothed in trousers whose perfect creases fell like a plumb line onto their turned cuffs. Only the knot of his tie was a little crooked, and examining him more closely, De Luca noted that Abatino's shoulders were a little sloped, and his stiff neck slanted forward a little.

"This is the second time they've kept us waiting at the door, poisoning us with toxic fumes," said Pugliese. "First that whore on via delle Oche, now here. It's true what they say, the police just don't count anymore."

Abatino's wrinkle tightened further, lengthening in the

direction of the corners of his mouth. De Luca was just in time to notice it.

"We have a lot to do today," said Abatino. "If this is something we can settle quickly, I'm prepared to answer your questions here, immediately. If more time is necessary, I will make it my business to come to the station tomorrow morning. With my lawyer, naturally."

"We have reason to believe," De Luca began, brusquely, "that one of your men murdered a photographer named Piras."

"What do you mean by 'one of my men'?"

"A man who works for you . . . for the Civic Committee, I presume."

"His name?"

"Matteucci Silvano."

"Never been a member of the Civic Committee."

"But you know him."

"I've heard his name."

"We have a film at the station that shows you together on a stage at a rally in Piazza Maggiore."

"There's always a lot of people at rallies, especially on stage. I don't remember that episode, I'm sorry."

In an effort to tear Abatino's answers out from the sound of the Lambretta, De Luca had moved closer with every question and by now he was close enough to watch Abatino's mouth. But this time the wrinkle didn't move, growing wide only when Abatino opened his mouth to speak. He realized that Pugliese was no longer by his side when he heard him cough, the sound coming from inside the garage.

"Jesus, fancy fucking safe you got built in here. And have a look over here, Commissario."

Through the fumes, Pugliese emerged from behind a row of cases stacked up against the wall. His eyes were watering and he was holding a rifle in his hand.

"It's mine," said Abatino, without turning. "I keep it here

because this neighborhood is out of the way and the street isn't even lit at night. Six months ago we were attacked by communists, and they sent everything up in flames."

"Sure," said Pugliese, "but this is no simple rifle. It's an automatic, a war weapon. It's not legal."

"This *is* a war. They have machine guns and cases of hand grenades hidden in the basements of the Casa del Popolo. Didn't you see what happened in Czechoslovakia? Didn't you hear Togliatti? If they win they'll give us all a kick in the behind with their hobnailed boots . . . So long freedom, so long justice, so long faith, so long family. Do you know what we do here, Commissario? This Civic Committee has a very special assignment . . . We organize counter-information to combat their strategy of disinformation. We defend the truth and we also defend you policemen who surely ought to know by now what side you should be on."

Now Abatino was breathing hard too, either because he'd gotten worked up over his speech or because the fumes were getting intolerable. All of a sudden, the Lambretta's motor died.

"She's flooded," yelled the boy.

"If you want to seize the rifle," said Abatino, once again impassive, "go ahead. If you want to arrest me for illegal possession, let me get my overcoat and I'll come with you."

"No," said De Luca. "I want to know if you knew Silvano Matteucci and if you know why he cut a photographer's throat and then turned his apartment upside down."

"I did not know him. He did not work for me. He was never a member of this Civic Committee. Is there anything else?"

"Why are you wearing a mourning pin?"

De Luca raised his finger and pointed at a black satin pin that Abatino wore in the buttonhole of his coat. Large and shiny, it was noticeable from a distance even against the dark fabric of his suit. Abatino swallowed and for the first time seemed human.

"The Honorable Orlandelli was like a father to me," he said. "More than a teacher, more than a spiritual and political guide. He was a saint. Am I under arrest?"

De Luca shook his head in silence. He turned and left the building, his hands in his pockets, his trench coat held tightly around him, and his mouth twisted into a grimace as he bit the inside of his cheek. Pugliese shrugged, leaned the rifle against the wall, and followed him out.

"A man of few words, Abatino, eh? What do you say, Commissa?"

De Luca didn't say anything. With his hands deep in his pockets, he kept walking, thoughtful, gazing at the ground. It appeared as if he were being careful to avoid the puddles in the asphalt, but instead he walked into the first one he came to, covering his shoe with water.

"Damn it," he muttered, pinching the crease of his trousers between two fingers and shaking the cuff.

"It's late and now that I'm my own boss I'm going to close up shop and head home for dinner," said Pugliese. "Do you want to join us, Commissa? I'll introduce you to my wife."

The hole in the street had been blown open by a grenade during the war. The shrapnel had marked the asphalt around the crater, like the claw marks of some gigantic animal. De Luca gazed down, biting his lip, then he looked at Pugliese.

"What do we have?" he asked.

Pugliese shrugged, embarrassed.

"Don't know," he said. "Soup, I think. Meat is still being rationed and this week—"

"What's meat got to do with anything, Pugliese? I mean the case. What do we have in hand? Still nothing . . ."

"Ah, sure . . ." Pugliese slapped his hand on his forehead,

VIA DELLE OCHE · 105

beneath the brim of his hat. "I thought you were talking about dinner. If you keep this up, Commissa, you'll end up making yourself ill."

They reached the portico and there the street was better paved. Pugliese tapped the soles of his shoes on the ground to get the mud off, lifting his coat up over his knees as if he were doing the flamenco.

"Well, I'm home," he said. "I live right over there. So what will it be, sir? Back to the station?"

"No. I'm going . . . somewhere else. I want to check on something . . ."

He waved goodbye to Pugliese, who stood watching him as he walked under the portico and then turned to shout, "My regards to your wife." His hands in his pockets, he disappearing around the corner.

"Predictions Based on Today's Sales of Election Lotto Slips in Rome . . ."

T his time even the door of number 8 via dell'Orso was closed, not just the windows, which by law had to remain so at all times. De Luca rapped on the door using the brass doorknocker, polished and equivocal, though not hard enough to "offend common decency," as Pugliese would have said. Then he slapped the door with the palm of his hand, then with the fleshy side of his closed fist. He stepped back a pace to look up at the windows, in vain, then heard someone calling him.

"Over here, Commissario."

Via dell'Orso was lit by a streetlight hanging over the road and another held to the side of a house by a wrought iron fixture, but De Luca still couldn't make out who had called him. He'd always seen her in sandals, la Tripolina, sandals and a slip, but here she was dressed, holding a little handbag with a blue scarf over her hair and tied under her chin. He told her so, too, when she got near enough:

"I've never seen you except in sandals and a slip."

"I'm wearing Notte di Venezia and a little Boise de Rose dress. Velvet Powder from Hollywood," said Tripolina. She raised her leg and propped her handbag on it, rummaging around for something inside. "A shame the shoes aren't Ferragamo. If they were I'd look just like a fashion model in

Grazia magazine. Now and again I get dressed up too, don't you know."

She pulled a key tied to a piece of string out of her handbag and opened the door. She pushed it open, waiting for De Luca to go in first.

"The house in via delle Oche must be making good money," De Luca said, standing where he was.

"If you look closer you'll see I sewed the Boise de Rose myself, with curtain fabric that I had dyed. And Notte di Venezia was a gift from a student who studied for his exams in my establishment."

"And via dell'Orso? Somebody give you that as a gift as well?"

The door had swung closed. La Tripolina pushed it open again then clasped her handbag tightly against her hips, turning sideways to slip between De Luca and the doorjamb. De Luca followed her in. She turned the dial on the light switch and a lamp hanging from the middle of the ceiling came to life, its light reflected in the mirrors and the gold leafing.

"We're not open yet," said la Tripolina, untying the knot of her scarf. "The new fifteen come in tomorrow."

De Luca sat down on the red sofa, sinking into the velour cushions, and spread his arms over the curved backrest. He gave a quick flick of his head to shake off the sudden feeling of exhaustion that always overwhelmed him at the most inopportune moments.

"I'm not a client," he said. "I'm here to ask some questions. Then we'll see whether the new girls arrive tomorrow or not."

La Tripolina had taken off her scarf. Her hair was still tied in a bun and a silken lock fell over her forehead, almost to her eyes. The Velvet Powder from Hollywood made her face a little lighter.

"Do you mind if I take off my shoes?" she said. "You're right, I'm used to sandals."

"Make yourself at home, it's yours, after all."

"Sure . . . Yours too, or so it seems."

She leaned down to slip the strap over her heels and kicked off her cork-heeled shoes. Her red knee-length dress had ridden up over her bare legs and she smoothed it out over her hips, De Luca watching her all the while.

"Why are all your girls saying the same thing? Who's been priming them?"

La Tripolina opened her bag and pulled out a transparent plastic bag containing something black. She turned it over in her hands, making it rustle, as De Luca continued to stare at her.

"What's your part in this game?"

"You know how I spend the little money I have, Commissario?" La Tripolina took a step toward the sofa. "I make my clothes myself. When I was a girl I worked in the revues and among other things I learned how to sew. But there's no two ways about it, stockings I've got to buy."

"What's your part in this game?"

La Tripolina opened the bag and turned her gaze, serious, insistent, to De Luca. "Do you mind if I try them on?" she said, quietly. She hiked up her dress and put her foot on the edge of the sofa, between De Luca's legs.

"No, no . . . wait a minute, Tripolina," De Luca said, stiffening. "Let's get things straight right from the start . . . I'm here to ask questions. I'm no customer. Questions, Tripolina. Have you ever heard of a certain Abatino?"

La Tripolina moved her foot forward, suddenly, coming so close to De Luca's trousers that he jumped. She had rolled one leg of her stockings up into a little black doughnut and, squeezing her toes together, she slipped it on, brushing against him once more. She pulled the dark nylon up over her leg and smoothed it out with her hands, pointing her toes and turning her leg sideways to straighten the seam with her fingers, from the reinforced heel at the base of the stockings to the top, which she held with both hands around her thigh, as she wasn't wearing a garter belt.

"Has it really been a year since you last touched a woman?" she murmured.

De Luca didn't answer. He sat there, immobile, his spine straight against the backrest, his arms open as if on the cross, watching her. He watched her as she pulled a hairpin from her hair, held it in her teeth to open it, and then used it to fasten the hem of her stockings to her panties. He watched her as she picked up her shoes and walked toward the staircase, one leg veiled in nylon and the other bare, shaking her hair loose as she went. Standing on the first step, one hand on the banister and her shoes hanging from the index finger of the other, her hair still bunched around the back of her neck, her dress hiked up revealing the dark tops of her thighs, la Tripolina looked back at De Luca over her shoulder and gestured toward the top of the stairs with a nod—an indecent nod, a whore's nod. De Luca sighed, took his arms from the backrest and stood up. Already halfway up the stairs, she stopped a moment to wait for him.

He woke with start. Someone or something had yanked him from his sleep and for a moment he lay there with his mouth open, blinking in the dark, asking himself where he was. The metal squeak of the bedsprings and the creak of the wooden bed frame told him he was in bed, and that he'd been sleeping. The sight of la Tripolina, panting, naked and wide-eyed on her knees at the side of the bed, told him that he had slept in via dell'Orso.

"Sorry," she said. "You scared me. I'm not used to having someone in my bed."

De Luca looked at her and she closed her eyes tight.

"I mean I'm not used to sleeping with someone in my bed. They always leave before that."

"I figured that's what you meant," said De Luca. "I wasn't thinking of that."

A faint light filled the room. Dawn slipped through the partially closed shutters and splintered the darkness of the room, sketching glimmering patterns of shadow and light on Tripolina's body. She was beautiful, thought De Luca.

"You're beautiful," he said, and she smiled. She slid back onto the bed, moving close to him. He felt her skin, warm and a little damp with sweat, against his side. She pressed her forehead against his cheek, put her arm over his chest and her fingers in his hair, still ruffled by the night's sleep.

"Listen . . ." De Luca had to make a small effort to remember her name, her real name. "Listen, Claudia . . ." At the sound of her name she pushed her forehead a little harder against his cheek. "Listen, Claudia . . . How is it that you . . . I mean, why did you . . ."

La Tripolina raised her head for a moment, then rested it back where it was, but a little higher on the pillow, her lips close to De Luca's. He felt her warm breath on his mouth.

"I'm sorry," he said. "A stupid question . . ."

"No," Tripolina said. "Just that I wasn't expecting it. It's the kind of question *talkers* ask. In bed, in brothels, you get your *tender hearts*, who want to be cuddled like their wives cuddle them; you get the *specials*, who want strange things; the ones who fall in love; and then you get your *talkers*, who want to talk afterwards. I wouldn't have guessed you were a talker."

"I'm curious by nature," De Luca said. "But it doesn't matter, forget about it. I . . ."

"When I was a girl I was working as a soubrette in the revues . . . I mean, I was a chorus girl, but I had promise. I danced with Wanda Osiris, but they fired me straight off 'cause they found me in bed with the MC, who was her boyfriend. I slept with him because he promised me a gift. Who knows, maybe I've always been a whore down deep. But it doesn't matter . . . If things go right for me, one day I'm gonna have a house like Chabanis in Paris, and then . . . *Ciao, Osiris!* And you? Why do you do what you do?"

"Maybe because I have always been a cop down deep. I'm curious. That's why I want to know how you fit into this . . ."

La Tripolina slipped her fingers out of De Luca's hair and placed them over his lips. "I've been in every brothel in Italy," she whispered through her fingers onto his lips, "even the high-class ones, where a girl learns things," her whispers caressing his eyes, his neck, "I can do everything, anything, I do it all, whatever you want . . ." his chest, his stomach muscles, which contracted beneath her warm breath, then down, further.

"Tripolina . . . Claudia, wait . . ." muttered De Luca. He closed his eyes, clenching his teeth with a groan when her lips touched him, and her tongue, flicking, then her teeth. He raised his head and caressed her naked back, shining under the dawn's light. With a sudden movement he clasped her shoulders, brushing against her hair.

"Claudia, please, wait, Claudia . . . Christ, Tripolina! You can't do this every time I'm about to ask you something!"

La Tripolina lifted her face and turned to look at De Luca. Hair stuck to her forehead, damp with sweat. She was kneeling on the bed and her face, caught between the rays of sunlight shining through the window, was in darkness. Nonetheless, De Luca could make out her eyes, which were half-closed, and her lips drawn tight.

"Why?" she said in a voice that was barely more than a whisper. "Why not? This is what I've always done. Leave me be. Leave me be and you can do whatever you want, whenever you want, with me, with my girls . . ."

"So, you do have a part in all this."

La Tripolina had already lowered her head again, putting her hand on De Luca's chest, but she lifted it suddenly and clenched her fist. She would have scratched him if her nails weren't cut so short.

"Tell me what's at the bottom of this story. If you're afraid, don't worry, I'll take care of it . . . I'll protect you, Claudia."

"You'll protect me?" She smiled, a harsh smile that made the wrinkles at the sides of her mouth return. "You're not that powerful, Commissario. Neither of us is. You're just a cop and I'm just a whore. And anyway, I've been protecting myself since I was twenty years old. I've made my offer. You know what you've got waiting for you here, you got a taste of it last night . . . And you liked it. What do you say? What do you say, Commissario?"

De Luca sighed and sat up. He swung his legs over the side of the bed and planted his elbows on his knees, running his hands through his hair. He didn't know what to say, so he kept his mouth shut and started to get dressed, in silence. He heard la Tripolina moving around behind him. It sounded like she had gotten off the bed, but he didn't have the courage to turn around. He felt embarrassed and tired, incredibly tired. When he had tied his shoelaces, still sitting there on the edge of the bed, he was momentarily overcome by the desire to fall back onto the still-rumpled, still-warm sheets. Then he shook his head and stood up. Only then did he turn to face her. La Tripolina was standing beside the bed, naked, her dark skin seemed to shine in the blades of dust-laden light coming from the window. She stared at him with that harsh look of hers, halfway between cynical resignation and a tremulous longing to cry.

"Ciao, Tripolina," he said and walked out of the room.

He had almost reached the bottom of the stairs when she looked out over the banister and yelled, "Dead duck, faggot, limp dick . . ." She threw a pillow at him and kept yelling until he had disappeared through the door.

APRIL 17 1948
SATURDAY

"IF ELECTIONS ARE NOT ORDERLY, THEY WILL BE DEFERRED."
"COMMUNISTS IMPEDE BILL-POSTING." "MORE WEAPONS IN REGGIANO."

"250,000 AT ROME RALLY FOR LIZZARDI AND TOGLIATTI. DEMOCRATIC FRONT WINS. HURRAH FOR THE PEOPLE'S VICTORY."

"ELECTIONS TOMORROW. TODAY, LAST CHANCE TO PLAY THE ELECTION LOTTERY. IT COULD CHANGE YOUR LIFE!"

When he got to the station he was limping because, along the way, he'd kicked a stone and hurt himself. At the bottom of the stairs, under the arch in the lobby, the night guard was still on duty. He saluted De Luca slowly, his eyes bulging with sleep and his hand heavy, hanging off the brim of his cap. De Luca didn't respond. He went straight to his office, his footsteps echoing in the hallway, uneven footsteps, a cripple's footsteps. He sat down in his swivel chair and held fast to the edge of his desk to soften the creak as he flopped back against the backrest. An almost perfect silence enveloped him. He closed his eyes and sighed deeply. In the length of that sigh, the entire office wrapped itself around him, as if it wanted to swallow him; the slightly pungent odor of stale Lysol, the dusty smell of file cabinets, the damp odor of wall paint, the sour reek of linoleum, even the strong oily smell of his pistol, which he had removed from the pocket of his trench coat and placed on the desk in front of him. He would have fallen asleep there and then, dulled by the smell of the stationhouse, but his chin was resting on his chest, and from his open shirt came a trace of a sweet, ever so slightly acidic, smell. Notte di Venezia, Hollywood Velvet, or perhaps just the scent of la Tripolina's dark, smooth skin. He sat up, leaned his forearms on the desktop and buried his head in his arms, overwhelmed, almost drunk on the smell of gun oil in his nose.

Di Naccio woke him up with a suffocated hiccup and the sound of a stack of green files slipping out of his arms onto the floor. De Luca looked up with a start.

"Oh God, Commissario . . . You scared me."

"And you me," said De Luca, screwing up his face. The sour taste of gun oil was on his lips and he could taste it in his mouth, penetrating down to the back of his throat.

"I didn't think I'd find you here," said Di Naccio. De Luca shrugged.

"I came in early this morning."

"I mean . . . I didn't expect to find you here, in this office."

De Luca was about to stretch, his arms open, hands bent back on his wrists. He stopped.

"Why?" he said.

"Because they've transferred you, sir. Didn't they tell you? I know they were looking for you yesterday, but . . . "

"Transferred? What do you mean transferred? Where?"

"I don't know . . . Night patrol, I think. They really haven't said a thing to you, sir?"

De Luca jumped up, picked up his pistol and put it in his pocket. At the door, he slipped on an 18C and to stop himself from falling he did a turn with Di Naccio, holding on to him, like they were dancing a waltz.

He ran up the stairs, two at a time, and stopped at the top to catch his breath, looking back down at the stairs that led from the field ops bureau to the upper floor, where the bureau chiefs had their offices. In front of him, the two doors were so near to one another and so similar that they could well have opened into the same office. The only difference was the words engraved on the nameplate: *Dottor Saverio Scala, Cabinet Chief* and *Dottor D'Ambrogio, Vicar to the Chief of Police*. De Luca's knuckles were against Scala's door, ready to knock the minute he got his breath back. But before he had a chance the door opened. Scala never changed: the same double-breasted gray suit, the same open shirt, no tie. Only the look in his eyes was different now, not quite as bemused.

"What's the matter?" he said. "I heard you running . . . What do you want?"

"I've been transferred," De Luca said.

"I know. Night patrol. But you can't complain; you're still in Bologna."

De Luca was lost for words. "They transferred me," he said once more, and then again, until the smile returned to Scala's lips; but it was a mocking smile, no longer bemused. De Luca fell silent, clenched his fists, and fixed Scala in the eyes.

"And the case?" he said.

Scala pushed open the door to his office, which until that moment he had held partly closed behind him, and stepped inside. De Luca stood in the doorway, disoriented. Scala's office was empty, with the exception of a cardboard box sitting on the desk with a stack of books and a green file sticking out of it. Scala walked over to the wall and unhooked a framed photograph. He tilted it away from the sunlight coming in through the window. Togliatti, Pajetta, Longo and Amendola crossing a cobblestone street, in conversation, and behind them, Scala, slightly out of focus, as if in the moment the photograph was taken he was just about to hop over the tram lines.

"The case doesn't interest anyone anymore, Commissario De Luca. We don't know where it might lead, and it's been decided that stirring up the dust right now would be a political mistake. I don't agree, but I accept the decision. My apologies."

He was about to put the photograph in the box, but De Luca grabbed him just above his elbow.

"What do you mean it doesn't interest anyone?" he growled. "It interests me . . . It interests us! We are policemen!"

"You, sir, are a policeman. I no longer am. It's back to politics for me, though I'd much rather go back to being a partisan. But I get the impression that the game has already been decided and that nobody'll be needing partisans anymore either. You know what our problem is, Commissario?" Scala took De Luca's wrist with two fingers and removed his hand from his arm. "We'd like to win, but we're afraid of winning too soundly . . . So, we end up losing, every time. By 'we,' I mean we communists, Commissario."

He dropped the photograph into the box then slid his fingers under the cardboard corners and lifted up the box. De Luca kept looking at him, letting himself be pushed to one side as Scala left the room.

"If you want to greet the new cabinet chief," Scala said, "you'll have to wait for Scelba to appoint him. But I'd suggest you present yourself to your new boss, Commissario De Luca. He's right here," he said, nodding quickly to the office next door, to the enameled nameplate on which was written *Dottor D'Ambrogio, Vicar to the Chief of Police.*

APRIL 18 1948
SUNDAY

"EVERYBODY TO THE POLLS. TWENTY-NINE MILLION ITALIANS CALLED TO DO THEIR DUTY." "WORLD ANXIOUSLY AWAITING ELECTION RESULTS." "AMERICAN AID: MARSHALL PLAN, $703.6 MILLION FOR ITALY IN FIRST YEAR."

"FOR ITALY, VOTE GARIBALDI!" "THE FRONT SOLEMNLY SWEARS TO RESPECT ELECTION RESULTS."

"POLICE: STRICT MEASURES TO ENSURE ORDER."

E asy, easy . . . Step back, please!"
The bed rocked as if it were afloat on the sea, suspended over the heads of the crowd gathered in front of the polling station. Lying on the bed, wrapped in a blanket, her head covered in a scarf and her hands grasping the edges of the bed frame, was a skeletal old woman, gazing about her, eyes peeled. De Luca signaled and three uniformed agents put their guns over their shoulders and barged through the crowd toward the bed, which was beginning to tilt sideways dangerously.

It was supposed to be an orderly queue, two by two, from the steps of the polling station to the corner of the street. And it had been, but then the hospital van arrived. What with all the stretchers and litters, and nurses helping down men wrapped in bandages, men with casts on their limbs, men dressed in pajamas, and police officers running here and there in an effort to help them, and hospital nuns who would have liked to vote immediately, but a group of men had formed a human cork at the door and one of the nuns even lost her headdress, and then four carabineri standing on the stairs starting to push back, and a woman with a child in a pram covered by a little umbrella beginning to yell, and De Luca raising his hand to the officers standing behind him, who clasped their weapons ready to fend off the crowd, what with all this, the queue had gone to the dogs. But then came the rain. Two drops. Two drops and no more. And everything stopped. The nuns got through and the queue reassembled itself into a clump, not orderly but calm, squeezed together in front of the door to the polling station, between De Luca's men and a pile of bicycles, on the ground, leaning against trees, up against the wall.

De Luca lifted his face, squinting up at the black sky, and a drop, a single drop, fell onto his mouth, tickling his lips.

"I'm going in," he said to a brigadier. He took advantage of a sudden breach in the crowd made by a woman who had opened her umbrella right at the entrance and ducked inside, slipping behind a soldier who was checking each person's voter registration form. The polling station was a public school. De Luca leaned up against a wall of the corridor, his arms crossed over his chest, looking into a classroom. A man sitting at a folding table was checking voter registration, a pencil in one hand and a salami sandwich in the other. He nodded to each person who came in, checked off his or her name on a list and took a bite of his sandwich. *Albertini Silvana*, tall, shapely, tight fitting gloves, and a bakelite handbag, white hat with a round brim and polka dot veil. Check next to her name and a bite of his sandwich. *Babini Uber,* short and ruddy, striped tie cinched tight around his neck, wavy hair stuck fast to his head with brilliantine. Check next to the name and bite of his sandwich. *Minzoni Matteo*, overcoat buttoned up over a pinstriped double-breasted suit, a triangle of white handkerchief sticking out of his breast pocket, check and bite. *Carloni Maria Grazia,* bent and twisted beneath her black shawl, an open handker-chief laid over her gray hair, like she was in church, check and bite. *Baroncini Vito*, ANPI[1] pin on the lapel of his unbuttoned jacket, *l'Unità* in his pocket, check and bite. Check and bite. Check and bite.

De Luca raised his eyes. The all too familiar feeling of nau-sea made his mouth twist. He looked over the head of the man with the sandwich to the window and the sky outside. A strip of blue had been torn in the black sky and in its midst there was a white cloud that looked like a dollop of whipped cream. De Luca would have liked to stick his head right in the middle of it, close his eyes and stay there for a million years, at least. Instead, he pushed himself away from the wall and stood on the tips of his toes to get a better look outside. A jeep from *Settimana Incom* [2] had just stopped in front of the building and a group of photographers and cameramen were jumping down onto the sidewalk.

"It's Dozza . . . Mayor Dozza has arrived," someone whis-pered. The corridor filled with people in a second and De Luca was cut off, pushed into a corner, his back against the wall. He tried to make room, to make his way through the crowd, his hands open, pushing apart shoulders, repeating the words, "Police, excuse me, police," but he was immobilized by a newspaper photographer who stopped in front of him, point-ed a camera in his face, and fired the flash, blinding him. De Luca closed his eyes. The flashbulbs going off intermittently turned the insides of his eyelids red. And it was then that he heard her, a woman, perhaps an old woman, lost in the middle of the crowd.

[1] *Associazione Nazionale Partigiani d'Italia* (Italian National Association of Partisans). Founded in 1944, the ANPI was created by veterans of the Italian Resistance. (Tr.)

[2] Milan-based newsreel service.

"Madonna mia, what a commotion, all these flashes. It's like a thunderstorm."

De Luca opened his eyes, wide, teary, and looked around. But he had already forgotten that voice and he was no longer thinking about Mayor Dozza, about the elections, and his assignment to maintain public order.

The thunderstorm. The lightning. A flashbulb.

"God, what a fool," he said aloud, and pushing his way through the crowd he left the polling station.

"AMERICAN AID FOR ITALY: $11 MILLION IN FOOD AND GASOLINE."
"SPIRITED ANTICIPATION FOR ELECTION RESULTS."

He wondered how she'd be dressed this time, sandals and a slip, or like a fashion model from Grazia, but when the door to via dell'Orso opened De Luca jumped back a step, surprised, because standing in the doorway was not la Tripolina but another girl. Blond, large firm breasts bound tight inside a corset with wire cups over which she had thrown a see-through nightdress, she was chewing, a breadcrumb on her chin.

"Not sure if we're open yet," she said. Looking back over her veiled shoulder, she yelled, "Signora, we open or not?"

"We're always open!" came a voice from within. The girl laughed, a quick, high-pitched laugh that blended with other cackles coming through the door from the round sofa inside. La Tripolina opened the door and came into the room with a tea towel in her hands. She was wearing a high-necked dress with small flowers printed on it that reached down beneath her knees and was tight around her hips. Her hair was tied in a bun at the back of her head, as always, and she was wearing slippers. She was still smiling at the answer she'd given, but when she saw De Luca she stopped.

"Ah," she said. "It's you. Get out of here, Dolores, I'll take care of it . . . It's for me."

She slapped the girl lightly on her behind and gave her the

tea towel. Then she leaned up against the door, one hand on her hip and her other arm extended along the doorframe, one bare foot against her knee. She stared at De Luca.

"What do you want?" she said.

"The truth," De Luca replied.

"The truth about what? You want to know how you fuck?"

"I want to know what happened in via delle Oche last Sunday."

La Tripolina swallowed, quickly, and seemed to sigh. But she didn't move. Her eyes were still staring into De Luca's.

"Nothing happened in via delle Oche last Sunday."

"Something happened, all right, something so big that Abatino had to kill three people. Something that could be photographed, from the back, with a flash, so that the person in the room on the courtyard could mistakenly think that there was a storm."

"Nothing happened in via delle Oche."

"You're under arrest."

La Tripolina moved back a step, as if suddenly unsteady on her feet. De Luca threw the door open and went in, leaving the slipper behind on the doorstep.

"I'm arresting you for withholding evidence, for being an accomplice to murder, and for violation of the laws on prostitution . . . One of the above, or all three, it doesn't matter. If you don't tell me what happened in via delle Oche I'll slap handcuffs on you and I'll take you in dressed as you are."

La Tripolina took another step backwards and pressed her lips together tight, so tight they turned white. Her chin was trembling and as she closed her mouth her eyes were full of tears.

"I told him he was too old for certain things," she said, with the hint of a smile, "and he didn't look so good, either, so pale . . . I've got a nose for certain things, I've been doing this job for a long time. But not him. He'd heard about Lisetta, he fancied low-class brothels and he liked his girls young. He wanted la Farrarese . . . "

"He who?" De Luca asked. But he was already breathing hard, because he knew who.

"So when Lisetta came down the stairs screaming I knew there was trouble. There he was in the room, dead as a door-nail, on Lisetta's bed . . . "

"Who, Tripolina? *You* have to tell me . . . Who?"

"The Honorable Orlandelli . . . Home and Church."

De Luca raised his eyes to the roof, a hushed oath on his lips, and smiled, while la Tripolina began crying in silence, large round tears rolling down her dark cheeks leaving her eye-lashes wet and shimmering beneath the light of the crystal teardrop chandelier.

"Now you're going to close me down," she murmured. "Now, right when I finally made it."

"No," De Luca said. "I mean . . . I don't know. It's not my decision to make . . . I'm a cop. Only a cop."

La Tripolina shrugged. De Luca would have liked to reach out and caress her cheek wet with tears. But he didn't. He didn't do anything except stand there looking at that girl cry-ing silently, with only one slipper on, and a dress with little flowers on it, closed at the neck, like the madam of a two bit whorehouse, until finally she turned and left the room, leaving her other slipper on the floor. De Luca left too, closing the door behind him and walking out onto via dell'Orso.

Number 16 via delle Oche had "gone dark" that Sunday. Special measures had been taken to ensure the utmost discre-tion. Even Ermes, the seraphi with links to the communists, had been sent away. But that didn't stop him from finding out that Chevalier Orlandelli, the Right Honorable Home and Church, would be coming there. It was probably Lisetta herself who told him, that tiny girl His Honor was coming to see in that dive of a brothel where you could get a "simple" for fifty lire. And Lisetta told him, not because she too was a communist but because it was a chance for her and Ermes to get away. Lisetta and Ermes! "Soon to be husband and wife" said the words on the photo that had been ripped from the cabinet. In the end, it was the only one of all those fake engagement photos that he'd held on to. Yes, one good photograph of the Right Honorable Home and Church in via delle Oche, coming out the door of number 16 after a "simple" or maybe a one-hundred-lire "double" plus a little added extra, was all they needed. And there was a photographer, too. Piras Osvaldo, son of Gavino, deceased, official whorehouse photographer, a good communist, sure, but when push came to shove more interested in money than the party. But the Right Honorable Home and Church had croaked. The only one left to negotiate with was Abatino, with his gang of former fascists, and maybe because he was a man used to action and not words, maybe because he didn't have the money, or maybe because those photographs of His Honor wrapped in plaid, stone cold dead in Bologna, in via delle Oche, and not seated in his office behind Piazza del Gesù in Rome, had become a commodity, a trump card with which to negotiate important favors, to be obtained quickly in order to stay afloat, maybe for that reason he had started killing people, one after another, and almost before they were even aware of him, until he found his photographs.

De Luca emphasized that the last part was his personal hypothesis, though very close to being a reasonable certainty. Likewise, another almost certain hypothesis of his was that la Tripolina really didn't know about the blackmail and the murders and that she had merely taken advantage of the situation, for which reason "the abovementioned may be considered guilty solely of the crime of concealment of a body and failing to report a death, in violation of the provisions of Article 7 of the Public Safety Act, 'Pertaining to Acts of Prostitution.'"

And then there were the charges against Dottor D'Ambrogio, accused of aiding and abetting.

When he got to the last line of the report, D'Ambrogio raised his eyes, his lips tight and a thin, crooked line in the middle of his forehead.

"Which is to say?" he said in his childish falsetto.

"Which is to say that Piras had been collaborating with OVRA as an informer since '29 and, since '47 with the chief of the political squad, that is, with you, sir. And while Ricciotti was dealing with Abatino and then lamenting the betrayal of his trusted photographer, Piras came to you to tell you what happened to the Honorable Orlandelli. Right before the elections. And you, sir, took excellent care of everything, shutting Tripolina up and scattering her whores throughout the country. But that fanatic Abatino got in first, before Piras could get the photographs to you. I can't blame him, really. Without the photographs Abatino would be out on his ass. Am I wrong?"

De Luca had been standing in the same position from the moment he entered the office and slapped a triplicate copy of the typewritten report down on D'Ambrogio's desk, his hands on the desk, the weight of his upper body leaning over them, his whole body perched, tense, like a vulture, his fingers clamped tight around the edges of the wooden desk. And now as he straightened up and stood back from the desk he felt a shooting pain his back. D'Ambrogio straightened up too, leaning against the back of the chair. He was tall enough to cover the bottom corners of the portraits of De Gaspari and Pope Pius XII hanging on the wall behind him. The plaster crucifix hanging a little higher up was safe. He wasn't that tall.

"Depends," he said. "You've been making one mistake after another since you got here, but there's always time to make good. What are you planning to do, Dottor De Luca?"

"I'm not a dottore."

"What are you planning to do, Special Sub Commissario De Luca?"

"Complete the investigation. Go directly to the magistrate to get the case assigned to me. Bring in all the girls from the previous fifteen at via delle Oche. Ask that an autopsy be done on the Right Honorable Orlandelli, and ask for a search warrant for via del Porto number 18, the headquarters of Abatino's Committee, because I'd bet my left arm the photos are there."

"You're already taking quite a gamble, Special Sub Commissario De Luca, not with your arm, I'd say, but with your head. In terms of your career, I mean . . . I'm no Abatino."

De Luca frowned and clenched his teeth. He crossed his arms over his trench coat.

"Are you trying to intimidate me, Dottor D'Ambrogio?"

"Mercy, no, Special Sub Commissario . . . I don't intimidate anyone. I am merely consulting with my very capable staff member about the possibility of following a lead in a very, very complicated case. Because those conclusions that you, with astounding presumption, define as 'certainties' are nothing more than hypotheses . . . Or worse, conjecture. What are the conjectures contained in this report based on, Special Sub Commissario De Luca?"

"The word of a prostitute whom I will not fail to name when the time comes."

D'Ambrogio pushed himself back in the chair, right back to De Gasperi, and stood up, unhurriedly. He went over to the window and looked out. The window looked down onto the piazza and even from there, from the third floor, it was possible to see at the end of the porticoed street, a cart covered in stacks of compressed paper. They were tearing the campaign posters off the walls.

"You know what this country needs?" he said, as if speak-

ing to himself, as if murmuring a few bars of a song to himself.
"Stability. This country needs to rebuild, not to destroy. Even
the other side figured that out. It needs a modicum of
respectability. It needs to shift world opinion in its direction, it
needs investment capital, it needs general Marshall's dollars,
and the Atlantic Pact . . . It needs order."

"Law and order."

"They're the same thing."

"Not for me. I'm a policeman."

D'Ambrogio turned his head and glanced at De Luca over
his shoulder. "So am I," he said. "And as such I work for the
government. Higher interests, Special Vice Commissario De
Luca, higher interests."

De Luca didn't say a word. D'Ambrogio sat down and
pushed the triplicate copies of the report toward the edge of
the table.

"Let's end this meeting here," he said, his voice becoming
even more high-pitched. "You may send your observations,
about which you very appropriately informed me, directly to
the magistrate. But I assure you, and in your heart of hearts
you must certainly know it yourself, they will forever remain
dead letters. Otherwise, you might want to follow the correct
chain of command and send your report onto your immediate
superior."

"Who might that be?"

"Me."

De Luca smiled and D'Ambrogio's cheeks reddened. He
placed two fingers on the copies of the report, pushing them
aside and making room for a stack of folders that were resting
on a corner of the table. He ran his fingers down the edges of
the folders until he got halfway. Then he pulled out an orange
folder. De Luca caught his breath.

"I was tidying up the staff files," D'Ambrogio said, leaning
over the file and squinting like he needed to look closer, "when

I ran across yours, Sub Commissario. 'High Commission For Expurgation,'" he read, "'personal file for Dottor De Luca etc., etc. . . . ' You see, here they call you dottore? But that's not the point. It's the questions . . . Member of the PNF? Yes, naturally, we all were . . . Political squad? No. March on Rome? No. Was one of the following included among duties . . . ? No. Member of the Volunteer Militia for National Security? No. Member of OVRA? No. No, no, no . . . Bravo De Luca. On the other hand, you were only a cop."

De Luca didn't respond. He was breathing with difficulty and his heart was beating hard.

"It's just that . . . well, the problems begin when we get to question thirty-two. Member of the Fascist Republican Party? Now, here you didn't give an answer and you didn't reply to any of the questions about the Salò period. Now . . . " D'Ambrogio raised his eyes and looked at De Luca, "we're clearly dealing with an oversight and we have no reason to doubt the responses you wanted to make, all 'no' I imagine, and I hope . . . If it weren't for this . . . "

He pushed another sheet forward and De Luca lowered his eyes as D'Ambrogio turned it around with a swift pirouette using two fingers so that De Luca could read it. It was a little square slip of paper, the back side of a ration card and it was marked with the blue stamp of the National Liberation Committee. It was typewritten. De Luca read the first few lines, before raising his eyes to D'Ambrogio's.

"It's fake," he mumbled, his voice as thin as a length of string.

"I have no doubt that you are not directly responsible for the facts attributed to your office," said D'Ambrogio. "Nonetheless, you still find yourself in a difficult position. If I'm not mistaken, your commander was tried and sentenced to death at the end of the war . . . Oh, of course, those times are over, thank God, together with those excesses of severity . . . I believe that these days you would get off with a rather light sentence. Obviously," now D'Ambrogio raised his eyes too, and fixed De Luca, "obviously you would be immediately expelled from the police force."

"No," mumbled De Luca, or perhaps he only imagined he had said something. D'Ambrogio pressed his lips together and shook his head, then he closed the orange file and put it beneath the others. The square slip of paper, typewritten on the back of a ration card, remained where it was, at the edge of the table. De Luca stared at it, panting hard, his fists tight at his sides, their knuckles white from the effort and his finger-nails digging into his palms. Then he snatched up the slip of paper, so fast he hardly touched it and left the office.

Outside, in the corridor, he put the square slip of thick paper into the pocket of his trench coat, with difficulty, as his hands were trembling. He clenched his teeth and began walking fast, then faster still, and an officer who had just come out of an office touched him on the shoulder and said: "Dottore, are you feeling ill?"

"No," De Luca said, his voice barely audible, "no, grazie." Then he burst through the door to the bathroom reserved for bureau chiefs, locking the door behind him, and turned all the taps on, as he was sobbing loudly and he didn't want anyone outside to hear him cry.

APRIL 22 1948 WEDNESDAY

"Absolute Majority for Christian Democrats. 207 Seats in the Chamber of Deputies. The Catholic World Exults in the Overwhelming Defeat of Communism."

"The Labor Confederation Will Collaborate with the New Government."

"New Talk of a Meeting Between Truman and Stalin."

"Election Lottery Winner to Be Announced Within a Week."

APRIL 26 1948 MONDAY

"Bartali Wins in Zurich Thanks to a Powerful Sprint."

MAY 14 1948 THURSDAY

"De Gaspari May Present the List of Ministers to President Einaudi Tomorrow."

"Marshall Plan in Force: Aid for Europe in First Twelve Months."

"President Einaudi's Message to the Pope: May the Holy Father Bless Italy."

"TODAY AT THE IMPERIALS, BOB HOPE AND DOROTHY LAMOUR: *MY FAVORITE BRUNETTE*."

MAY 16 1948 SUNDAY

"AND NOW THE HOLY LAND IS IN FLAMES. WAR IN PALESTINE AN INTERNATIONAL THREAT. LONDON PERPLEXED, MOSCOW STIRRING UP THE WATERS."

MAY 20 1948 THURSDAY

"KREMLIN'S PLAN: AN ENORMOUS STALINIST EMPIRE STRETCHING FROM THE ELBE TO THE BEARING STRAIT. THE FIRST REACTIONS FROM MOSCOW TO WHITE HOUSE REFUSAL."

MAY 22 1948 SATURDAY

"RUSSIAN-AMERICAN TENSION REMAINS. EUROPE ARMED TO THE TEETH TO AVOID THIRD WORLD WAR."

MAY 29 1948 SATURDAY

"PRICE OF GRAIN REACHES 6,000 LIRE. RATIONING OF BREAD AND PASTA CONTINUES. BUT DEREGULATED SALE OF SUGAR PROBABLE."

"TODAY AT THE ARENA DEL SOLE: *THE KING'S COURIER* WITH ROSSANO BRAZZI AND VALENTINA CORTESE."

"GINO BARTALI: AS LONG AS I STAY CLOSE TO COPPI NOBODY CAN COUNT ME OUT."

JUNE 24 1948 THURSDAY

"DANGEROUS DEVELOPMENTS IN THE COLD WAR. TITO VERSUS STALIN? RUSSIAN BASES IN THE BALKANS."

"SERIOUS DISTURBANCES IN NAPLES: TWENTY-SIX OFFICERS OF THE LAW AND FIVE CIVILIANS INJURED. SCELBA SPEAKS TO THE CHAMBER: THERE CAN BE NO DEMOCRACY WITHOUT DISARMAMENT."

"TODAY AT THE ARENA DEL SOLE: JOHN LODER, JUNE DUPREZ: *THE BRIGHTON STRANGLER*."

JUNE 30 1948 WEDNESDAY

"TOUR DE FRANCE BEGINS TODAY IN PARIS."

JULY 1 1948 THURSDAY

"BARTALI WINS THE FIRST LEG OF THE TOUR DE FRANCE."

JULY 8 1948 THURSDAY

"BARTALI VICTORIOUS AT LOURDES, DEFEATING ROBIC AND BOBET IN A SPRINT."

JULY 9 1948 FRIDAY

"BARTALI WINS AT TOULOUSE IN A SPRINT."

JULY 10 1948 SATURDAY

"BARTALI, THE CLIMBER WHO BECAME A SPRINTER."

JULY 14 1948
WEDNESDAY

W ord is Togliatti's been shot."
"Come off it, what kind of joke . . . "
Pugliese stood up—Brigadier Bartolini was never one for practical jokes. He had run inside, losing his hat as he came through the rattan curtain hanging in the doorway of the Maldini Café. He'd found everybody there: Maresciallo Camelo, with a ham sandwich in his hand halfway to his mouth, Brigadier Maranzana, with his mouth wrapped around a mortadella panino, Commissario Zecchi, who raised his eyes over the rim of a glass of bubbling light white.

"Half an hour ago . . . in Rome," he sputtered, reclaiming his hat, which hat fallen down onto the back of his neck. "A university student shot Togliatti as he was coming out of Montecitorio!"

"Fuck's sake," muttered Pugliese. "Is he dead?"

"I don't know. The chief of police wants to see us all, right away! There's gonna be a revolution!"

They left together accompanied by the noise of chairs being scraped across the floor and the click-clack of the rattan curtain, Maranzana with his mortadella panino still in his hand. Only Pugliese stayed behind. He walked around the counter and started hammering against the door of the bathroom with his fist. De Luca was spitting into the hole of the Turkish john, his mouth twisted by one last heave, useless and parched. It

was the same story whenever he tried to eat. Or most of the
time.

"Commissario! Come on out, sir! They've shot Togliatti!"

"Minister of the Interior Scelba has issued categorical
orders that any form of demonstration of whatever type shall
be stopped. I repeat: categorical orders!"

Chief of Police Giordano was standing on a chair waving
around a wire message printed on light blue paper. The briefing room was full of bureau chiefs and uniformed officers,
several detectives in uniform, all of them packed in tight,
sticky with sweat and red-faced from the July temperatures
and the closed windows. Whenever anyone went to open a
window the chief of police yelled for them to stop. At first De
Luca asked himself why, then a second later he too found himself standing like all the others, struggling for air, worried and
scared.

"CGIL has called for a general strike! In Genoa the demon-
strators are disarming the police and carabinieri! We've got
unrest in Turin and Milan! Piazza Maggiore is jammed with
people! The piazzas are coming to a boil!"

He had even stopped smoothing back his hair, had Chief of
Police Giordano, and his bald pate, polished with brilliantine
and sweat, glistened where his ruffled comb-over left it bare.
Shoved up against a blackboard that was dirtying his jacket
with chalk, D'Ambrogio clapped his hands together to call the
crowd back to attention.

"The important thing is not to lose out heads!" he cried.
"All department heads and non-commissioned officers have
been reassigned to public order posts! Use of weapons only
when necessary! Don't lose your head! Don't lose your head!"

The jeep was waiting with its motor running, packed with
officers, and Pugliese was standing on the running board hold-

ing down the backrest of the front seat. De Luca came running over, grabbed hold of the maresciallo's arm and jumped in, breathing hard.

"They're moving in from via IV Novembre!" he gasped. "They want to blockade the station! Go! Go!"

The officer in the driver's seat ground the gears. The jeep leapt forward with an evil growl and they drove out of the courtyard of the prefecture. De Luca was holding on to the spare tire, virtually lying on top of the officers of the riot police who, their feet hooked under the seat bottoms, swayed right and left as the jeep rounded the curves. Pugliese, hugging the backrest of the seat in front of him, held his hat down on his head with one open hand.

"Jesus, Commissa," he groaned. "The revolution has arrived!"

Via IV Novembre was full of people running in every direction. The jeep carrying a squad of riot police cut through the crowd fast. People veered out of its path like crazed flies. The officers leaned out, their arms raised and their batons clenched in their hands, upside down so that they could strike with the grip, and swung. There was a low wall halfway down the street, a few meters away from a cluster of loose paving stones, that a group of people were knocking down with an iron bar. A second later Pugliese let out a yelp as the windscreen of the jeep shattered and the officer at the wheel pulled hard left, running the jeep up onto the sidewalk.

"Down! Down!" De Luca cried as he leapt over the spare tire. He was almost struck by a brick that bounced off one of the tires, and then by another that left a dent in the body of the jeep, and then another, and then by chairs and tables from the bar on the corner of Via de' Fusari. "Madonna mia," Pugliese moaned as he dragged himself out from under the dash, his back covered in shards of glass. Behind the jeep, an officer was sitting on the sidewalk holding his bloodied head and another officer was kneeling, his gun drawn, aiming it wildly in the direction of the crowd.

"No!" De Luca yelled. "No!" Then somebody fired two pistol shots. The officer returned fire. Then the riot boys opened fire with machine guns, firing above the crowd's heads, at their feet, at the walls, wherever. The crowd dispersed, splitting left and right and then went wild and charged again.

Everything was closed, everything was still. The shops were shut, their shutters drawn over the display windows and their doors barred. Trams and cable cars had been abandoned in the middle of the street. Trains sat immobile on their tracks. The great hall of the station was crowded with people who had been caught off guard by the unexpected strike. They were sleeping on the floor, leaning up against their bags. It was almost evening, but it was still hot.

In front of the station, sitting on the jeep's running board, Pugliese was eating from a mess tin. His spoon scraped against the bottom of the tin. Every time he lifted the spoon to his mouth he would lick it clean with a swift, discreet slurp. And whenever he did so, De Luca frowned, irritated.

"Are you sure you don't want something, Commissa? There's enough for you, too. I'll have them bring you—"

"No, thank you."

De Luca was sitting in the driver's seat, his knees up, his legs jammed against the steering wheel and his head resting on the top of the backrest. The day's stress and that unnatural position was wreaking havoc on his back and the hard ring of the steering wheel was cutting into his legs, blocking his circulation. But he didn't have the strength to move.

"Commissa," Pugliese said, putting the spoon in the mess tin and placing it on the jeep's round fender, "in your opinion, what'll happen if he dies? A revolution?"

"No," De Luca said. "There'll be no revolution in Italy. The

Marines are all set to land at Livorno, and even the communists know that. They'll reach an agreement."

"Yeah, but I mean as far as we're concerned . . . I mean, we're fucked."

"Yes, we're fucked."

"Zecchi says that they took seventeen officers to Sant'Orsola hospital this morning. He reckons we arrested at least two hundred people today. They set fire to the headquarters of the Uomo Qualunque and tore apart the headquarters of the Monarchists and the MSI. At Piazza della Marcanzia they attacked the security guards protecting the headquarters of the Liberal Party. What the fuck was this guy, the shooter, Pallante, thinking? Togliatti!? He'd even been in a seminary."

"Like Abatino."

"Can't manage to forget him, eh, Commissa?"

De Luca tried to shrug, but a shooting pain in his neck made him jump. He lifted his head, slowly, forcing his sore muscles.

"No," he said. "I can't forget him. He's no longer secretary of his committee. He's got an office downtown now and nobody knows exactly what he does. But they still have the warehouse, and the dogs, and there's someone guarding the place 24-7, and I'm convinced that they've still got the photographs in there somewhere. Right there, in via del Porto, in that wall safe."

De Luca remembered the furnished room that he had been renting for a month. First he'd been living in via Saragozza, in a pensione, like a student. It was close enough to the station and he only went there when he decided it was time to try to sleep. But then he had started seriously looking for something better, talking with his colleagues and barkeepers until he found another place, a bare room with a bed and three pieces of dusty furniture. The entrance was on a narrow street with a ridiculous name, via Strazzacappe, but the window . . . the window looked down on via del Porto, where Abatino's civic committee had had its headquarters. On the chest of drawers beside the window there was a square slip of paper, a ration card. It had sat there for three months now without being moved. His stomach tightened painfully and growled loud enough for Pugliese to hear.

"Don't let it poison your blood, Commissa. If I were you, I'd worry about that mania you have for not eating. It may be some kind of nervous disorder . . . No offense, of course. As for me, I've come to terms with it . . . When I do my duty, I'm satisfied, Commissa . . . "

"We didn't do our duty, Pugliese!" De Luca sat up and lowered his knees. "He's not in jail! He's not in jail!"

He rubbed his legs, which had suddenly been invaded by millions of biting ants. Pugliese watched him without saying a word. Then both of them turned because a violet police Guzzi was coming down the street with an officer standing on the foot peddles waving a white-gloved hand in front of his face.

"Here we go again," said De Luca. He slid over to the passenger seat to leave room for the driver and the other officers, who jumped into the jeep, their batons in their shoulder belts.

JULY 15 1948
THURSDAY

"This Morning at 9 a.m. Bulletin no. 7 Regarding the Condition of Comrade Togliatti Was Issued: Mean Maximum Body Temperature, 38°C; Pulse, 120bpm; Respiration, 32; Blood Pressure 125/70. General State of Health Reasonably Good."

He was dreaming of la Tripolina and the last time he'd seen her, by chance, at the stationhouse. He was walking past the offices of the vice bureau; usually he turned the other way, uneasy, but that morning he happened to glance in. He saw her from behind, her hair tied in a bun beneath a round hat, the collar of her suit jacket sticking up from behind the back of the seat where she was sitting, and her ankles crossed beneath the chair, with one stockinged heel suspended above her little stilettos. He didn't stop. He pretended not to have noticed her and perhaps she had done the same, because as he walked on, his gaze fixed ahead, he heard her chair creak, as if she had turned around. A little later, at Maldini's, Brigadier Di Naccio told him that she had sold the license to via dell'Orso because she was heading off to open a brothel in Argentina. De Luca nodded.

The minute he woke fully, however, he forgot all about her. The windows of his room had torn him from of his sleep, vibrating violently like they were about to break and leaving the fleeting sound of an explosion in his ears. Then there was another, coming from far away, on the other side of the intersection with via Marconi, at the end of via del Porto, this time dull and rapid. The sound made him pull his head down

between his shoulders with an instinct that he still hadn't forgotten. It was the sound of a hand grenade.

"Police! Commissario De Luca! Police!"

The officer raised his machine gun when he saw De Luca
running toward him with his coat open and flapping around
him, only one sleeve on and the other hanging, weighed down
by the pistol in his pocket. At the end of via del Porto, amid the
clouds of tear gas, it was possible to make out an overturned
jeep and officers hidden behind a truck, firing on something.

"Communists," said the officer. "They wanted to close a
hosier's that was still open for business and when we got here
they threw everything they could find at us from the windows
of the school across the street."

"And the bombs? Who threw them?"

The officer shrugged.

"Us, them . . . Who knows? Somebody threw them. Three
injured . . ."

De Luca nodded. He looked around, quickly, and the
minute he saw what he was looking for he touched the officer
on his arm and turned.

"Commissario De Luca," he said to the brigadier, who was
crouched behind the door of a Fiat 1100. "Turn on the radio,
you'll have to call for reinforcements. And find Maresciallo
Pugliese, look for him at home. Tell him to come down here."

"Why?" said the brigadier. "The riot squad is here, they're
rushing the agitators, and it looks like everything will be over
soon."

"Do you talk back to your superiors?" said De Luca, hard,
and pointed at number 18. "Do you know what that is? A
Civic Committee headquarters. Call for reinforcements. We
need to draw a line of defense."

"Commissa, sir, you're out of your mind."

"No, Pugliese, I'm a police officer and I am executing my duties to the letter. We've got a possible communist objective here. And I want to enter before they attack it. What I find there is my business."

"And you think you'll get away with it, Commissario?"

The officers went to work with the butts of their rifles, and with a loud snap, the metal gate gave way. De Luca walked into the courtyard, his pistol in his hand, but the dogs and the guard had vanished. A brigadier broke a window, cursing the minute he saw the iron bars behind it.

"Nobody's getting in here," he said, but De Luca was already pointing his pistol at the door.

"Look out!" he yelled. He emptied his clip against the lock, then he and some officers threw their weight, shoulders first, against the splintered wood.

The garage was empty except for the papier-mâché Garibaldi abandoned in a corner beside a little trapdoor built into the trampled earth. On the wall, jammed tight into the crumbling wall plaster, was the safe. It looked like the door of an oven, closed by a slab of painted metal with three locks and a dial. De Luca stood there in front of it, staring, biting the inside of his mouth.

"Mamma mia, Commissa," Pugliese complained from behind him. "They finally sent us off for a bit of rest this morning, and now . . . C'mon boys, open up here, we might have some communists hiding inside."

The problem, thought De Luca, was to find a legal way of opening the safe. The problem was to blow off the door to the safe without his search being so clearly unlawful that the evidence would be compromised. Because he knew, he felt it clearly, that inside the safe were those photographs, the ones that had kept Abatino afloat. If not, why all the surveillance?

"Commissa . . . come over here, now, please! Commissa . . . please, down here!"

The trapdoor concealed a smaller room, a tiny space dug into the earth but big enough to contain two rows of stacked crates, Pugliese in their midst, and De Luca who, at Pugliese's cry, had come down a short wooden set of stairs that looked like those in front of a chicken coop. He had to bend down a little, because he was the taller of the two men. He hit his head on the roof, though, when Pugliese made him step aside, out of the light that was shining on the one crate he had opened.

"Rifles, Commissa . . . automatic rifles, all well oiled and nice and new, the carabinieri flame stamped on the butt. And that stuff there, wrapped up like that . . . those are explosives. There's enough here to arm a small covert army, Commissa. What is this stuff? What is it?"

It was dark in the hole but De Luca could see that Pugliese had turned pale. He leaned over the open crate and ran his fingertip along the oily gun barrel, then rubbed his greasy fingertips together. Then he turned brusquely and ran up the little set of stairs.

He thought he would have to break down another door. He thought he'd be breaking into another empty office, the file cabinets overturned and the charred remains of documents lying in the fireplace. He thought he'd have to call in and get a search warrant wired out for Abatino Antonio, a.k.a. the Little Abbot. Instead, he found him in his office. Abatino Antonio, known as the Little Abbot, was on the telephone.

"Put down the telephone or I'll shoot!" cried De Luca from the doorway, his pistol aimed. The Little Abbot raised his arms, the black bakelite receiver in one hand. He looked at De Luca from behind the opaque lenses of his glasses. He was pallid and a corner of his mouth was trembling.

"They want you," he said.

"They want me?" De Luca said. "What do you mean, they want me? Who is it?" He lowered his pistol and walked

toward the telephone, hesitantly. Pugliese had entered the
room. He put his hand on Abatino's shoulder as De Luca took
the phone from him.

"Commissario? Chief Giordano here . . . Commissario, can
you hear me?"

De Luca nodded, dazed, then cleared his throat.

"Yes, sir, chief . . . I hear you."

"Dottor Abatino called me to turn himself in. He confesses
to having ordered those murders three months ago . . . The
ones you investigated with such laudable zeal . . . Do you hear
me, Commissario?"

De Luca nodded again, then again he cleared his throat.

"I hear you, sir."

"Well, then . . . I'll leave my congratulations on the case for
another time. For now, your orders are to arrest Dottor Abatino
and bring him to the station, where he will be handed over to
the appropriate bureau. Do you understand, Commissario?"

"Yes," said De Luca, this time aloud. "Yes, but there's a
store of weapons that . . . "

"All in due time, Commissario, all in due time . . . First
things first. This business is homicide's concern now. The
investigation will be passed over to dottor Bonaga who will
soon be asking you for a suitably thorough report on the matter. Your job is to bring the suspect here with the utmost dis-
cretion. The situation is under control now, but prudence is
the order of the day Commissario De Luca. Prudence!"

"I'll be out in a year. Like Cippico."

"Monsignor Cippico is a con man, Abatino. You're a murderer."

They held him between them, their shoulders touching.
They had thrown his coat over his shoulders so as to conceal
the handcuffs. The 1100 was not far away, but they had to cross
the street and walk another hundred meters in the open.

"Political crime . . . committed at a very particular moment. I'll blame that idiot Matteucci . . . And then, I know people. You have no idea the people I know. A year so that nobody remembers me anymore and I'll be out. You'll see, policeman, you'll see . . . This country forgets quickly."

The Little Abbot spoke in spurts, a hint of anxiety in his voice, but with resolve, as if he were attempting to convince someone of what he was saying, maybe himself. De Luca, on the other hand, didn't say a word. His face dark, his teeth sunk deep in his cheek. Then he saw them, a group of men who had come around a corner fast. De Luca, Pugliese, and Abatino stopped dead and stood there, shoulder to shoulder. Six men, maybe seven, were coming toward them. The group was still too far away to make out each man clearly in the dark, but their voices were loud, excited, and one of them was even waving his closed fist in the air.

"Shit," said Pugliese.

The Little Abbot took a step back but De Luca held him by one arm and Pugliese by the other.

"No, no . . . this lot will kill us," whined Abatino. "They're communists . . . They found out, they've seen us. They'll lynch me!"

"By the looks of them, they'll lynch all three of us," said Pugliese. "What do we do, Commissario?"

"What do we do? I don't know, Maresciallo. I don't know . . . "

They took out their pistols and held them down, hidden behind their hips, their fingers tight around Abatino's stiff, trembling arms and their eyes fixed on the group as it got nearer. They could make them out now. Seven men. Wound up real good. One with his fist in the air, yelling something. Suddenly he leapt forward in their direction. He took two steps and stopped, raised both arms hard and fast like he was hammering the air above him.

"Bartali's got the yellow jersey!" he cried.

Pugliese dropped his pistol. De Luca didn't move. He was breathless. The Little Abbot began laughing, a thin hysterical laugh that made his chin and his lips, wet with little wads of spit, quiver.

"I'll be out in six months," he said.

They've made me Chief Maresciallo, they gave me a raise and now they're sending me to Sicily to hunt down the bandito Giuliano. On the force, they call this 'promote and make remote' . . . You know all about it, Commissario."

De Luca smiled and nodded quickly. Pugliese smoothed down his raven hair, shiny with brilliantine, then put his cap on with a swift precise movement, pushing it back off his brow. They were on the stairs that led up to the bureau chiefs' offices.

"I going to grab a ride from a colleague and go home and pack my bags. Tomorrow evening I have to be in Palermo."

"I'm sorry," De Luca said. "It's my fault."

"Forget about it, Commissario. Things went even worse for you."

De Luca lowered his gaze and bit his lip. Pugliese leaned out over the banister and looked down to the lobby. "I'm coming. Just a second for fuck's sake," he called, raising his hand.

"The investigating magisrate is in Giordano's office," De Luca said quietly. "They should be calling me in at any moment. In your opinion—"

"Yes," said Pugliese. "In my opinion they'll put you on trial, Commissa. The story was everywhere. This morning it was even in *Carlino* . . . as they call the *Emilia Times* now. It was small but it was there and easy enough to notice . . . "

Easy enough to notice, indeed. Two quarter columns side by side, in the local news. But the headline was in bold. It grabbed readers' attention. "Police Officer Slips through the Purge." Nothing compared to the second page of yesterday's *L'Unità*. "Who Is Commissario De Luca?" next to a photo of him with his hands in his pockets and a black shirt under his trench coat, and in italics, short but strong, "A Just Punishment."

"Well," said De Luca. "I reckon it was bound to happen sooner or later . . . "

"I'm coming!" Pugliese shouted, leaning over the marble balustrade. "Fuck you, fella, I'm saying goodbye to a friend!"

He turned back to De Luca and opened his arms wide. "Maybe they won't do anything to you, Commissa," he said. "It may only be a way to get you to keep your mouth closed. And in my opinion, sir, you ought to keep your mouth closed. I've been in the force for a long time and I know that there are cases you solve and cases you don't. We solved our case, Commissa. We cuffed him."

"Right." De Luca smiled. "We cuffed him."

"Oh, for God's sake, what a fucking pain in the ass . . . I'm coming!" Pugliese took De Luca's hand and held it firmly, shaking his arm. "Time to say goodbye, Commissa. Good luck . . . from the heart, De Luca, really. From the heart."

He lowered his cap on his forehead and ran down the stairs, and it looked to De Luca, from the movement he made with his arm, though his back was to him, that Pugliese had wiped one eye dry with the back of his hand. But there was no more time to reflect on it because from the top of the stairs an officer was calling him, clapping his hands together like a schoolmarm. He waited impatiently for De Luca to reach the top of the stairs and then pointed to a small velour sofa next to the door to the chief's office and there De Luca sat, his hands on his knees, his head against the wall and his eyes closed, waiting for them to call him in.

Carlo Lucarelli is one of Italy's best-loved crime writers. He was born in Parma in 1960. His publishing début came with the successful De Luca Trilogy in 1990 and he has since published over a dozen novels and collections of stories. He is an active member of several Italian and international writers' associations; he has taught at Alessandro Baricco's Holden School in Turin and in Padua's maximum-security prison. He hosts a popular series on network television entitled *Blu Notte*, which deals with real-life unsolved Italian mysteries. This is his third book to be published by Europa Editions. *Carte Blanche*, book one in the De Luca Trilogy, was published in 2006, and its follow-up, *The Damned Season*, was published in 2007.

Now Available from Europa Editions

A

Amazing Disgrace,
   James Hamilton-Paterson

B

Between Two Seas,
   Carmine Abate
The Big Question,
   Wolf Erlbruch
Boot Tracks, Mathew F. Jones
Broken Colors,
   Michele Zackheim
The Butterfly Workshop,
   Wolf Erlbruch

C

Carte Blanche, Carlo Lucarelli
Chourmo, Jean-Claude Izzo
Cooking with Fernet Branca,
   James Hamilton-Paterson

D

The Damned Season,
   Carlo Lucarelli
The Days of Abandonment,
   Elena Ferrante
Death's Dark Abyss,
   Massimo Carlotto
Departure Lounge,
   Chad Taylor

Dog Day,
   Alicia Giménez-Bartlett

F

Fairy Tale Timpa, Altan
Fresh Fields, Peter Kocan
The Fugitive,
   Massimo Carlotto

G

The Girl on the Via Flaminia,
   Alfred Hayes
The Goodbye Kiss,
   Massimo Carlotto

H

Hangover Square,
   Patrick Hamilton
The Have-Nots,
   Katharina Hacker
Here Comes Timpa, Altan

I

I Loved You for Your Voice,
   Sélim Nassib

J

The Jasmine Isle,
   Ioanna Karystiani

Visit our Web site for complete information on these and forthcoming titles.